D0352329

Halfway House

Eleanor Davies

Scripture Union

By the same author:
Designer Label
In the Spotlight

Copyright © Eleanor Davies 2002
First published 2002

Scripture Union, 207–209 Queensway, Bletchley, Milton Keynes,
MK2 2EB, England.
Website: www.scriptureunion.org.uk
Email: info@scriptureunion.org.uk

ISBN 1 85999 556 X

All rights reserved. No part of this publication may be repro-
duced, stored in a retrieval system, or transmitted in any form or
by any means, electronic, mechanical, photocopying, recording or
otherwise, without the prior permission of Scripture Union.

The right of Eleanor Davies to be identified as author of this
work has been asserted by her in accordance with the Copyright,
Designs and Patents Act 1988.

British Library Cataloguing-in-Publication Data.
A catalogue record of this book is available from the British
Library.

Printed and bound in Great Britain by Cox & Wyman Ltd,
Reading, Berkshire.

Scripture Union is an international Christian charity working with
churches in more than 130 countries, providing resources to bring
the good news about Jesus Christ to children, young people and
families and to encourage them to develop spiritually through the
Bible and prayer.

As well as our network of volunteers, staff and associates who
run holidays, church-based events and school Christian groups,
we produce a wide range of publications and support those who
use our resources through training programmes.

*For Elizabeth,
in memory of Katherine,
and for all my friends at 'The Bank'.*

1

If old Reg Tanner hadn't died that autumn, the Big Mac incident might well have put an end to Encounter, the St Michael's youth group.

It wasn't that its members wanted to stop going, nor was it that any of them had fallen out – at least not apart from Sophie Illingworth and Michelle Smith, and they were always falling out so they didn't count – nor was it because the numbers had dropped off. In fact it was exactly the opposite: it was because the group was so big that the problems arose. The truth was that no one had a house big enough to contain them all. They tried going to a different home each week in an attempt to spread the load among the parents; but it was always the same: there was not enough room to do anything except sit like tightly packed sardines, taking it in turns to breathe and using up as little space as possible.

Jamie and Laura Bevan lived in quite a big house compared with many of their friends. Their living room was reasonably spacious, so it was a good place for the group to meet. Unfortunately, Clare, their mother, was so fussy about mess that the extra size of their house tended to be cancelled out by the amount of parental moaning that went on after a meeting of the group.

'I don't really see how we can go on much longer without somewhere proper to meet,' said Jamie to his sister as they waited for the group to arrive on a Sunday evening early in November. The evenings were getting darker and darker, it had turned very cold in the last few days and the long light summer days spent mooching in the park were nothing but a distant memory.

'I know. Although I suppose there's always the church hall, as Ben keeps pointing out.'

'Yeah, right,' said Jamie, making a face. 'All those plastic stacking chairs and ancient brown flowery curtains and that manky disinfectant smell. And it's so cold. And you have to clear everything away every time you go in there because of the playgroup.'

'But p'raps it'd be better than nowhere,' said Laura without much enthusiasm.

'Not if we want new people to come. Can you imagine taking a friend from school to that hall on a Sunday night? They wouldn't stay a minute.'

Laura sighed. 'Well, let's think about it later. We've got this evening to worry about now. What are we doing this week?'

'Not sure. Ben's in charge. I think he's got something planned. He said he and Noah might be a bit late, something about seeing the vicar.'

Ben, a Jamaican-born social worker, was the leader of Encounter and his eldest son Noah was their closest friend. It was unusual for them not to be on time; Ben usually arrived early to get things organised for the evening.

The doorbell started to ring and young people began to pour into the Bevans' house, laughing and shoving each other until every square inch of the living room was full of bodies.

'…twenty-one, twenty-two,' counted Jamie. 'And I don't think they're all here yet. Where can Ben and Noah be?'

Clare was hovering at the door behind him, peering into the room from the hall.

'I hope there aren't any more,' she said, 'there's nowhere to put them. It'll ruin my suite, people sitting three in a chair like that.' She scowled at three girls who were tightly wedged in one armchair, all talking at once at the top of their voices, quite oblivious to her disapproval.

Jamie fidgeted, trying to suppress his irritation. 'It'll be fine, Mum, don't worry. We'll come and get you if there's a problem.'

'Hmf. And who's supposed to be in charge of you all? Isn't there supposed to be an adult here? Where are Fred and Jane?' Fred and Jane were a young married couple who usually came along to help Ben.

'They couldn't come tonight, but stay cool, Ben'll be here in a minute. It's all under control. I'll be responsible.'

'That's what worries me,' said Clare drily, but her attention was diverted by another ring on the doorbell. It was Michelle Smith, bearing a paper bag embellished with a familiar pair of golden arches.

'Oooh! McDonalds!' squeaked Sophie Illingworth from the depths of the armchair. Disentangling herself from a pile of arms and legs, she launched herself across the room at Michelle. 'Give us a bite!'

'Get yer own,' was Michelle's brief reply as she unwrapped a large squashy hamburger dripping with sauce and gherkins and sank her teeth into it. Jamie watched in despair as several bright red drops fell on the pale blue living-room carpet, but his mother had disappeared to the kitchen. Perhaps he would be able to sneak a damp cloth in later and clean up the marks before she saw them.

'Don't be such a meanie!' whined Sophie. 'Go on, give us some! Or at least a few chips!' She stretched out a hand towards the hamburger, but Michelle was too quick for her and snatched it away, holding it high in the air.

'Gerroff,' she said, waving it tantalisingly above her head.

'Oh Michelle, do be nice. You're so stingy. I shared my crisps with you at dinnertime last week, have you forgotten?'

But Michelle had chosen to forget. She managed to find herself a space in the corner next to the television and sat cross-legged on the floor, munching. Furious, Sophie clambered over the bodies between her and Michelle, scattering a pile of magazines off the coffee table, and landing heavily on the shin of a yelping boy who was sitting in the way.

Michelle looked round wildly for somewhere to put the hamburger out of Sophie's reach, but she was trapped in a corner. It was then that she caught sight of the grey plastic flap which covered the gaping slot beneath the television, just the right width to take a hamburger; a place where Sophie's thieving fingers couldn't reach. As Michelle explained later, she knew in her head that it wasn't a very sensible thing to do, but it was just that in the heat of the moment it seemed like the easiest place to put it. Deftly, she posted the burger, all squelchy with ketchup and mustard, into the video recorder.

An uneasy hush descended on the room.

'Nice one, Michelle,' said one of the boys rather nervously. No one else said anything.

Laura and Jamie exchanged glances. Both knew what the other was thinking: once their mother had found out, they'd never be allowed to have the youth group round again. Should they go and tell her now, Jamie wondered, or wait till everyone had gone home? If they told her now maybe she would be less angry than if their friends weren't there, but on the other hand she might make a terrible scene in front of everyone.

In the silence the doorbell sounded extra loud. Ben and Noah had arrived.

'Sorry to be so late,' said Ben breathlessly, 'I had to go and talk to the vicar about something very important – something that involves all of you, so it had to be tonight.'

He looked round the unusually quiet room. 'Is anything the matter?'

'No, nothing,' said Jamie hurriedly. Now was not the moment for confessions. 'Tell us what you had to go and see the vicar about.'

Ben sat on the arm of the sofa then, hearing an ominous creak, appeared to think better of it and stood at one end of the room with his back to the window.

'How many of you knew Reg Tanner?' There were a few positive murmurs.

'He was the guy that owned the Halfway House wasn't he, the pub on the hill? Didn't he die a few weeks ago?' said one of the boys.

'He was nice. I liked him,' said Gemma, a friend of Laura. 'He often used to stop and talk to us when we were waiting for the bus. I was well gutted when he died.'

'Well,' said Ben, speaking slowly for maximum impact, 'Reg's will has just been made public and guess what he's done? He's left the pub to us!'

A pause, then a buzz of questions.

'Us? What do you mean, us? He left it to Encounter?'

'That's right. At least, he left it to the church but with the suggestion in his will that our group should have first refusal.'

'But why us?'

'What would we want with a pub?'

'Isn't it rather dark and smelly?'

'Reg really left the place to the church in his will?' said Jamie in disbelief. 'What did he think we'd do with it? It's a bit wacky leaving a *pub* to a church, isn't it?'

'I guess it's not a normal thing to do,' agreed Ben, 'but he had no relatives left after Sybil died and most of his friends were gone. I suppose the church was his family. He only started coming to St Michael's when he was in his seventies, and he was so amazed at the warm welcome he got from so many people that he came up with this way of thanking them when he died.'

'But why us? I mean the youth?' said Laura. 'Surely there are lots of other things it could be used for?'

'Nothing more deserving,' said Ben. 'Look at you now, all squashed up together. There just isn't room for all of you in people's houses.'

'True enough,' said Jamie, 'people have actually stopped coming 'cause it's such a crush.'

'Exactly,' said Ben, 'and haven't we often said how we wished we could start a drop-in club in Stanworth like the one at the Methodist church in Trigton? But we never had the place to do it. There's a whole stack of kids out there with nowhere to go, some of them with big, big problems. I see them all the time at work, kids who need a friendly ear, or maybe just a place to chill out. We've got the church hall, of course—' he was interrupted here by a clamour of groans, '—OK, I'm the first to admit it's not the trendiest venue in town. Anyway it's always being used for Keep Fit classes and Brownies and that sort of thing.'

'So you're suggesting we turn the pub into a kind of coffee bar,' said Laura slowly, clearly warming to the idea. 'A sort of place where anyone of our age could just drop in after school or on Saturdays or something.'

'Well, it'd need a lot of organisation,' said Ben, 'but yes, that's the general plan. We'd have to get adults to help run it, but there's no reason why some of you kids couldn't help with serving behind the bar and that kind of stuff. So, what do you think?'

No one spoke for a moment, each waiting for someone else to be the first to react, then Gemma said decisively, 'I should think it's obvious, isn't it? We need to go and have a look at it.'

'I thought you'd say that, so I've arranged for a few of you to come down there with me tomorrow evening after school. Can I suggest Jamie and Laura, Clicker, Gemma and Noah? You five have been involved in the group the longest. Would the rest of you be prepared to go along with their opinion?' There was a general murmur of agreement.

Naturally, after that, Ben's carefully prepared programme for the evening had to be abandoned; nothing could be as interesting as discussing the new club.

It wasn't until the last person was leaving that Laura pointed out to her brother that they still had to tell their mother about the hamburger in the video.

'Smell-ee,' said Jamie, wrinkling up his nose and breathing in the dank atmosphere.

'And damp,' said Laura, eyeing the streak of black mould which crept up the wall behind the bar.

'And a truly hideous colour scheme,' added Gemma.

The walls and ceiling of the room were a deep shade of coffee brown. Whether they had been painted that colour originally, or whether they had become stained from years of cigarette smoke and spilt drinks it was hard to say, but it seemed unlikely that in its present state the pub would feature in *Homes and Gardens*.

'But just think what we could do with it!' Noah was looking round the lounge, his eyes sparkling. 'We've even got a ready-made bar to serve drinks from. And look at the window seats – they're dead cosy. Can't you just see us all in here? And, hey look, fruit machines!'

'Sorry, the fruit machines are going,' said his dad, 'you don't think we'd encourage gambling in a Christian youth club do you?'

'S'pose not. Bummer.'

'But I'm hoping to replace them with some sort of computer type games if we can find the money. We might be able to keep the darts, if I decide that you guys can be trusted with such lethal weapons. And maybe a pool table, but again that depends on cash.'

'Yeah and we could have table tennis, too, in the other lounge!' shouted Jamie who had been exploring the other end of the room. 'There's a door here through to it; the room's quite a bit smaller but there'd still be space for a table.'

Gemma was looking at the floor. 'Carpet's a bit yuck,' she said distastefully, poking at the splodgy patterns with a fashionably booted toe. 'It smells all musty. Seems to me like there'd be a load of stuff to do to get it nice. But I s'pose if Ben'll help us… you would help us, wouldn't you, Ben?'

'Of course,' Ben replied. 'I brought you here because I wanted you to be the first to see it. I knew if you could see its potential you'd be able to get your mates to come and help do it up. I know it's a bit of a dump at the moment, but as Noah says, all we need is some imagination and we could make it really good. It couldn't be in a better place, all the kids pass this spot after school every day. So what about it? What do you think, Clicker? You haven't said anything yet.'

Clicker was wandering around in an abstracted kind of way, prodding the rough velvety covers on the chairs and watching little clouds of dust billowing out.

'Yeah.' He pushed his glasses up his nose. 'S'good. I like the computer games idea, too.' Clicker's real name was Alexander, but he spent so much time closeted with his dad's computer that his friends had renamed him.

Ben went on, 'It'd be a club that'd really attract all those kids who would rather die than set foot inside a church, a kind of halfway house between the world out there and St Michael's—'

'Halfway House? But that's the name of the pub,' interrupted Laura in hushed tones. 'How totally spooky. It's almost as if it was *meant*…'

There was an awed silence as the friends gazed at each other.

'I guess that settles it, then,' said Jamie briskly. 'We'd better get to work as soon as possible. How do we go about it? And who's going to pay for all the re-decoration?'

'Can we choose the colours and everything?' asked Gemma, doing an excited little dance on the spot. 'I've got so many great ideas about how we could do it! We could make it all sort of night-clubby, with those low lights and things—'

'Hey, hang on a minute,' Ben held up a restraining hand. 'What we have to do is come up with some sort of plan and then take it back to the finance guys at church and see if there's enough money. See, the thing is, although Reg left us the building, he didn't leave us a bean for doing it up. I reckon as far as he was concerned there was nothing wrong with it. So St Michael's has got to find the cash themselves. That means fund-raising.'

'Oh no, not car washing again,' groaned Noah.

'No, son, you don't understand, this kind of thing needs serious money. You'd all be seventy yourselves by the time we earned enough by car washing. No, what we've got to do is sell the idea to the church and then see if we can have a gift day and get people to just give the money straight out.'

'But would they just give it to us? Just like that?'

'They might. 'Specially if we use our secret weapon.'

'Secret weap–? Oh, you mean talking to him up there.'

'Sure. If this thing's going to be a success we're gonna need God on our side.'

Gemma shivered. 'Well, I don't know about anyone else, but I'm freezing. I think I've spent long enough here. Anyone coming home?'

'What do you expect if you insist on wearing that tiny little T-shirt in the middle of November?' Laura gave Gemma her most middle-aged look, the sort of look mothers give at daughters who put sexiness before warmth.

Gemma was unconcerned. 'It was warmer when I came out,' she said vaguely. 'Anyway I haven't got a jumper that goes with these trousers. So when are we going to put this plan together, Ben?'

'How about Sunday, our usual club night? At our place?'

'Cool. I'll bring a paint-chart.'

The trouble with Gemma, thought Laura, as she brushed her teeth before going to bed, is that she's completely away with the fairies. All she thinks about is how she looks and who she wants to go out with. If things were left to her, nothing would ever get done. Fancy going out dressed like that when it's practically winter. If Ben hadn't taken us all home in the car she'd probably have died of exposure.

She swallowed a glass of water and winced. It was so cold outside that the water coming through the pipe into the cold tap was only just above freezing, and she could feel its icy journey down through her insides. She scooped her clothes off the bathroom floor ready to return to her bedroom but stopped as she met Jamie at the door.

'I hoped it was you in there,' he said. 'I've got something to show you. I had an idea for the new club. Do you want to come and see?'

'OK,' said Laura, 'but I must get to bed soon, I'm completely wiped out. Make it quick.'

She followed him across the landing into his bedroom, her towel over one shoulder. His room was bigger than hers, with a window which looked out onto their back garden and also gave a good view of the neighbours' gardens on both sides. Anyone going in there for the first time would know instantly what his hobby was; every available wall space was covered with photographs. Black and white, coloured, large, small, places, animals, birds, people. His ambition was to become a professional photographer, and every penny he saved went towards photographic equipment.

'Well?' said Laura.

He pointed to his bed. Laid out on the duvet were more photographs, pictures of people and places they both knew.

'You know that big wall in the pub, the one on the right of the bar with no windows or door in it? Didn't you think it looked really boring?'

'I don't know,' said Laura trying to remember, 'I suppose I just thought it was a wall. Why?'

'Don't you think it would be brilliant to make a sort of collage – a collection of pictures of local people and places – a sort of celebration of life here where we live? All in photographs? We could add in new people as they come to the club so that they feel part of the place. It'd be the first thing you'd see as you came in – can't you just imagine it? I might even swing it so that it could be part of my GCSE project. And Dad would help with the developing and everything.'

Laura had no doubt that he would. Clive Bevan taught art at the school they both went to, and it was he who had got Jamie so interested in photography. It was all part of the father/son bonding thing that kept niggling at her and made her feel faintly irritated with Jamie much of the time. She knew it was a bit bizarre that she should feel this way, considering her dad was an embarrassingly bearded remnant from the Sixties who had only recently cut off his pony-tail, and who had a worrying tendency to say things like 'groovy chick' and 'far out daddyo,' when her school friends were around. But the fact that the men in the family were both so arty was hard to bear, since she herself hadn't got an artistic bone in her body. In fact, Jamie was always falling about laughing at the way she couldn't even keep inside the lines when shading in maps for geography homework. Really, if she was honest, her brother was good at just about everything that went on at school. In the choir, in all the dramatic productions and in half the teams, and as if that wasn't enough he bore a scarily strong resemblance to Zac, lead singer of Strawberry Corner, the boy band currently topping the charts. Whereas she was just plain uninteresting old Laura, all right at most things, but nothing special at anything.

'It's not a bad idea,' she said, thoughtfully fingering the pictures, 'only you'd have to make them much bigger. These are too small to be seen unless you get really close.'

'Yeah, that's what I thought,' he said excitedly, 'and I could do people in their natural environment, like Noah out on a run, or Clicker in front of a computer screen.'

'Or Gemma in front of a mirror,' Laura couldn't resist adding, although she regretted it almost immediately.

'That's a bit harsh. You're not very nice about Gemma are you?'

'I know, I know. We're good friends really; it's just that sometimes she narks me. I think this is a great idea – suggest it to Ben. I'm sure he'll go for it.' She smiled at her brother, noticing that his face looked very pale in the glare of the bedside lamp. 'You look as tired as I feel. It's been a wild couple of days. Definitely bedtime.'

'Yeah, yeah,' said Jamie absently. 'I think I might just dig out a few more pictures before I go to sleep.' He was already rummaging under his bed and pulling out cardboard boxes stacked with old photos. She knew it would be another hour before he would finally turn out his light.

'Don't let Mum see you still up,' she warned, picking up her towel. 'She's still on the rampage after the McDonalds thing. You don't want her to stop us getting involved with the new club.' The memory of both her parents sitting on the floor poking inside the video recorder with coat hangers and a long handled dish mop was unpleasantly fresh in her mind, not to mention the blatantly unnecessary things they'd said about her friends.

2

It was nearly the end of February before work was able to begin in earnest on the new club. First all the legalities had to be sorted out, then all sorts of church committees had to spend hours discussing whether it was a suitable place for teenagers to hang around in; wouldn't it perhaps be more sensible to sell it and use the money raised from the sale? No, Ben had said, sitting patiently through all these meetings, the pub was exactly what Encounter needed, even if they sold it they would never find anything as good again. Then the building had to be checked for structural safety, efficient insulation, proper wiring and adequate plumbing. All this before a single penny had been raised to pay for new decoration and fittings.

'If we have to wait much longer we'll all be too old to get any benefit from it,' complained Clicker.

'Don't worry,' said Noah cheerfully, 'we can always use it as a Senior Citizens' Lunch club.'

Towards the end of January St Michael's held a Gift Evening. Ben was invited to explain to the church exactly what Encounter were planning to do with the new building. With the help of Jamie and Laura's dad he produced a huge drawing of the ground floor of the pub showing all the different activities they were hoping to provide and how they would be laid out, then the congregation were invited to ask questions.

'These computer games. Are they a good idea? Aren't they a bit addictive?' asked Sophie's mum. Laura, sitting on the back row amongst her friends, felt Clicker wriggling with suppressed irritation in the seat next to her.

'Not if we regulate their use,' said Ben calmly, 'in fact computers actually encourage creativity. We won't just use them for games, we're hoping the young people will use the Internet to look things up for school work, and perhaps do some activities like writing or computer artwork.'

'What about safety?' asked Jane Foster, the St Michael's playgroup leader. 'How many adults are you going to have in there?'

'Yes, and what about noise?' asked someone else. 'Is there going to be lots of loud music disturbing all the neighbours? How will you handle that?'

'No problem,' replied Ben, 'we've talked to all the people in the road and nearly all the buildings in the immediate vicinity are shops – the owners will actually welcome the extra trade the club will bring. There's a sweet shop on one side and a video shop on the other – both are places where the young people will want to go. And apart from the video place they'll be shut anyway when the club is open for evening activities. As for safety, we will of course always have adults in there to oversee things, and we're hoping for volunteers from the church.' He looked round his audience expectantly.

'Well, I think the whole thing sounds brilliant,' said a voice suddenly from near the back. It was Joanne, Gemma's mum, bouncing Gemma's baby sister Jodie up and down on her knee, very pink at being the focus of attention. 'I shall come and help if I can fit it round work hours,' she added, rather defiantly. She was a nurse and her duties made it very difficult for her to come to church; when she did she always crept in late as if she was afraid that people might object to her presence.

There were a few murmurs of approval from round her and a 'me too,' and 'I could probably manage the odd night,' from another corner.

Ben grinned at Gemma's mum. 'You're right, Joanne, it *is* brilliant. We are very fortunate to be in this position and we would be mad to miss such an opportunity.

'So—' he took a deep breath, '—so I do hope that many of you will feel able to support us financially.'

A collection followed. A large number of people wrote out cheques on the spot while others made promises of what they thought they could give. It was even better than Ben had hoped for. By the time all the promises of money had been added in, as well as the actual donations made that evening, there was enough both for the initial decorating and to buy nearly all the equipment they had talked about.

'Isn't it amazing?' bounced Laura to Jamie, when she got home and told him all about it. 'Even Mrs Potts said she'd make a contribution, in spite of the fact that she thinks anyone between the age of ten and twenty is the Devil's Spawn. Someone up there must be on our side. After a few objections they were all nearly as excited as we are!'

Jamie tried to look enthusiastic. He was suffering from a horrid bug which he couldn't seem to shake off, and hadn't felt well enough to go up to the church with Laura. In fact he'd had a really bad winter for illness, first a sore throat with a high temperature, then some kind of tummy thing and now another fever which wouldn't go away. He'd woken up that morning feeling very tired and achey and Laura's bounciness made him even more exhausted.

'Ben says we'll be able to start work by the end of the month,' went on Laura, 'there'll still be a builder and an electrician in there but he reckons we can work round them. With any luck we'll be able to open in early summer. Isn't it great?'

'Great,' agreed Jamie, wondering how soon he'd be able to get back to his photography. He hadn't taken any pictures since Christmas and he would need to get a move on if he was going to produce a folder in time for his exam in the summer.

But apart from a few annoying nosebleeds Jamie was almost back to his old self again by the last Saturday of February. That was the day when decorating began in earnest, and he was well enough to join the gang as they started work.

Although, it didn't really feel much like proper work, thought Laura as she rubbed one of the walls with sandpaper, more like an extended party. There were about ten of them there helping. Ben and their dad Clive were in charge, and two or three other dads and mums had come along as well, including Gemma's mum and stepfather Steve, who had left the baby with Laura's mum. Noah had brought his stereo and a collection of CDs, and the team of workers added a noisy cacophony of tuneless voices to the music as they began to scrape and scrub every surface in sight. Laura was wearing one of her brother's oldest rugby shirts and an ancient pair of jeans, her long mousy hair tied up in a piece of string. Gemma worked beside her, attired in ridiculously impractical white trousers.

'How much of this sand-papering are we expected to do?' she enquired, rubbing away delicately at a spot where a thick lump of yellowing paint had caked itself onto a skirting board.

'We've hardly started,' said Laura, sneezing from the dust which rose from the wall, tickling her nostrils. 'We've got to sandpaper the whole place and then wash down the paint-work. And all the wallpaper on those two far walls has to come off.' She waved her scraper at the far side of the room where Noah and Clicker had just deposited a large bucket of water on the floor, ready to start soaking the walls.

Jamie stopped by them on his way past to collect some more sandpaper and flicked some water with his thumb and forefinger at Noah as he passed. Noah, grinning, retaliated by hurling a large sponge into the bucket with a huge splash, drenching Jamie from head to toe.

Jamie laughed delightedly. 'You're gonna regret that!' he warned. He picked up the sponge from the floor, dipped it into the bucket, and without squeezing the water out threw it back at Noah. A full-scale water fight ensued.

Ben stepped through from the other lounge and just missed receiving a wet missile right in the middle of his face.

'Hey, guys, what're you doing? This isn't going to get the place looking good. Come on, get a grip. I was hoping you'd have that section of wall done by now.'

Jamie looked a bit shame-faced and returned to his work, but not before Noah had muttered from the side of his mouth, gangster style, 'Don't think I'm through with you yet, punk. Be afraid, be very afraid.'

The morning flew by and at midday they paused for lunch. Laura had finished sanding her section of wall and Ben called her over.

'Go and get us all something from the bread shop up the hill, will you?' he said, rummaging in his pocket for a couple of notes and some loose change. 'Pies or sandwiches, or whatever you like. And something to drink.'

Laura pulled on her old fleece over her grubby jeans and went out into the street. The sunlight outside made her blink after the dark interior of the pub. Standing on the pavement she could still hear the deep throbbing beat of Noah's CD player inside the building and the raucous sound of her friends' voices singing along. Her dad had begun work with his electric drill in the entrance hall where there was going to be a row of coat hooks, and the singers increased their volume in a vain attempt to drown out the noise.

She had only walked a few yards when she found her way blocked by a group of youths outside the sweet shop next to the Halfway House. There were four or five of them, big lads, several of them smoking, a couple drinking out of cans, silently standing and watching her as she approached.

Laura's heart skipped a beat. Should she ask them to move or should she walk round them? She would have to go onto the road in order to make a detour, and traffic was roaring past at an alarming rate. Or should she just turn round and run back into the pub?

Stay cool.

'Can I please pass?' she said politely to the nearest boy who was lounging against the wall of the sweet-shop, his black-booted feet stuck out in front of him in such a way that she could only get past by climbing over them. He said nothing, but smiled. Not a very friendly smile.

'I have to get to the baker's up the hill,' she said, furious at the sound of her squeaky little voice, and wishing desperately that Ben or her dad would come out and help her.

The boy smiled again. He had a chubby face, his right cheek bulged with something he was chewing and there were traces of something pink and sticky round his mouth.

'Vinny, boy, what can you be thinking of?' said another of the boys lolling next to him; a shortish youth, quite stockily built, sporting a natty number one haircut. He gave his companion a shove. 'The lady wants to get past! You mustn't get in her way.' He turned to Laura, clearing a space on the pavement and waving an arm to indicate her freedom to go through. 'I'm so sorry about my pal, he has no manners at all. Where exactly did you want to go?'

'The bread shop,' said Laura in an even smaller voice.

'The *bread* shop,' said the youth as if she had just stated her intention to go for a ten-course meal at the Ritz. 'The *bread* shop! She wants to get something to eat! And we stand in her way! How cruel is that? She might *die* of hunger, mightn't she, lads?'

The chubby boy sniggered. 'Hey, Lee, p'raps if we ask nicely she'll get us something too. I'm starving.'

'Great idea, Vinny,' said his friend, scratching his stubbly head and pretending to ponder. 'Now, what would be nice? A cream cake possibly? One of those fat chocolatey ones? Maybe some pasties and a big home-made pizza? Or perhaps an apple doughnut?'

'I—I haven't enough money to get you anything...' began Laura, but Lee grabbed the corner of her fleece and shook it, jangling the coins which Ben had given her.

'Funny. I wonder what that noise is. What've you got in here?' He thrust his hand into her pocket and pulled out a fistful of money. 'Hey look, guys, look at this! Jackpot day at the lottery! Well, whaddya know? Here, look after it, Robbie.' He counted it out and passed it to a boy with hair bleached at the tips, then pushed his face up close to hers. 'I think you could share it don't you? After all there's only one of you and there's five of us.'

'But it's not just for me,' quavered Laura, 'I have to get lunch for all my friends as well.'

'Aaah,' said Lee tenderly, 'd'you hear that, lads? She has friends. Isn't that touching? Where are they, then?'

'In there, in the pub,' she said. Surely when they realised how close her dad was they would leave her alone.

'In the pub, eh?' said Lee suddenly looking interested. 'The Halfway House? Well, then, perhaps you can tell us what's going on in there. All that noise and people going in and out. What are they doing to it?'

Laura took a deep breath. She was torn between a desire to turn round and run and a foolish urge to tell him about the project.

'It's going to be a club,' she said, 'a place for young people. Somewhere to go and play pool and listen to music and stuff like that.'

'A club, eh? And who's going to be allowed in it, then?'

'Anyone,' said Laura, 'anyone at all as long as they're the right age and' – bravely – 'don't cause trouble.'

'What, even people like us? Even me f'r instance?' said Lee with an evil grin.

'Yes, yes, anyone,' said Laura rashly.

'How much does it cost to get in, then? And who's going to pay for it?' he said scornfully. 'Who's going to pay for me to come into a club and have a good time?'

'It won't cost anything,' replied Laura, 'it's all supported by St Michael's – the church at the bottom of the hill.'

There was a burst of laughter at this.

'Unlucky!' said one of the boys.

'Tough, Lee, you gotta be a Christian!' added another. 'Don't forget yer Bible!'

'Better say a prayer for me, while you're there, 'cause you won't catch *me* dead in there!' threw in Vinny.

'Look out, lads!' came a sudden hiss from Robbie, the boy with bleached hair who'd been selected to look after the money. 'Someone coming!'

Alerted by the noise Ben and Clive had come out onto the street to see what was happening. In just a few seconds the crowd of youths melted away.

'What on earth's going on?' said her dad. 'Laura, are you all right? Who were those boys?'

'It's OK Dad,' said Laura, 'they've gone. Only they took the lunch money…' Her knees had gone wobbly and she battled with a stupid need to burst into tears.

But before the words were out of her mouth, Robbie magically reappeared from an alleyway between the newsagent and the florist, holding out a handful of coins.

'Here's your money,' he said hurriedly, 'take it quick!' He thrust it into her palm and raced after his friends.

Ben started to chase him, but he had already disappeared into the maze of little lanes that made up the back streets of Stanworth. It was easy for anyone who wanted to hide to dive into a shop or a doorway. Before long Ben gave up and rejoined Laura and her dad on the pavement outside the newsagent.

As he returned Clive was saying, 'I'm sure I know that boy from somewhere.'

Laura was searching her memory. Suddenly she said, 'I know who he is! Robbie King! Don't you remember, Dad, he was in the year above me at primary school and he used to come to the youth group when it first started. I just didn't recognise him with his hair a different colour.'

'Of course,' said her dad, 'I knew I'd seen him before. Well, that makes things easy, I know where his parents live, I can go round and tell them about the kind of company he's keeping.'

'No, don't do that,' said Laura quickly.

'Why on earth not? Look at the state you're in – they really upset you. We can't let them get away with it.'

'But he did bring the money back. I think he was sorry – it wasn't his idea to take it. Let's just forget it.'

'But surely—'

'I think Laura's right,' said Ben. 'If she doesn't want to pursue it perhaps we should let it rest this time. After all, these are exactly the sort of kids we are hoping to attract to the Halfway House.'

'Yes, but not if they're going to go round scaring innocent young girls in the street,' replied Clive. 'What would have happened if we hadn't been there?'

'But you *were* there,' said Laura, 'and that's what matters. Anyway, if I'd realised Robbie was one of them, I wouldn't have been such a wimp. They're only Jamie's age after all, and who'd be scared of Jamie?' Reassured by her own show of bravado she added, 'Can we go and get that lunch now? I'm about to collapse with hunger.'

Her father looked unhappy, but ignoring him, Laura set off up the hill, the two dads following behind her like a presidential bodyguard.

By the time they'd bought a selection of sandwiches and hot pies and returned to the Halfway House her legs had stopped feeling like jelly and she felt in control of things once more. The rest of the workers, blissfully unaware of what had been going on outside in the street, were sitting on the filthy carpet waiting for their lunch. Ben doled out paper bags to everyone till they all had something to eat.

'I think that's the lot,' he said; then, 'Oh no, I have one more pie here. Who ordered a pasty? Have I counted wrong?'

Everyone looked round.

'Where's Jamie?' asked Noah. 'I think he ordered a pasty.'

'Perhaps he's in the toilets,' suggested Gemma, without much interest. She'd perked up a lot now that she was in possession of a large cheese and pickle roll.

Clicker was nearest the door marked Gents. 'I'll go and look,' he said, and disappeared through the entrance.

'So what took you so long getting our lunch?' Gemma asked as Laura sank down on the carpet beside her. 'I thought you were never coming back.'

'Just a load of plonkers blocking the way,' explained Laura nonchalantly, she wasn't going to let Gemma see how scared she'd been. 'But, hey, I could handle them. One of them was Robbie King, do you remember him from primary—' she was interrupted by an urgent shout from the Gents' toilet.

'Someone quick! Jamie's having a huge nosebleed! It won't stop – someone come!'

Clive looked up from his sandwich. 'That's the third nosebleed he's had this week. I wonder what's causing them.' He reached for his coat and, pulling out a clean handkerchief, went into the toilets.

A few seconds later he emerged. 'Can you come and help, Joanne?' he said quietly to Gemma's mum. 'Jamie's fainted.'

3

It was Monday morning. Jamie settled back onto the hard green padded bench, trying to avoid the plastic squeak which accompanied any sudden movement, and stared at the height chart stuck on the wall of the surgery waiting-room. The chart was about four foot high, obviously designed for primary school children, and the ruler was designed to look like a ladder. Next to the measuring bit was a picture of a giraffe, neck extended, looking as if it would take a bite out of the head of any child who dared to get as tall as the highest rung. On the opposite wall another poster extolled the importance of regular teeth-brushing. Two impossibly shiny children, a boy and a girl, beamed out at the inhabitants of the waiting-room, their dazzling white teeth set in permanent smiles of joy. Just to look at them made you feel depressed, thought Jamie, who had had to make a real effort to get out of bed at all that morning.

His mum, sitting next to him, smiled encouragingly at him and he shuffled along the bench a little further away from her. However much you like your mum in theory, it doesn't do to be seen out in public with her. As if you can't go to the doctor on your own, but have to have her there to hold your hand. Although, if pressed, Jamie would have had to admit that deep down he was very glad of her company, in spite of her tendency to talk on his behalf as if he was only six.

The truth was, he was a bit frightened. To begin with, he hadn't worried at all about the way he'd kept getting ill over the winter, after all doesn't everyone get bugs in the cold weather? He'd just had more than his share this year. The worst thing was that he couldn't seem to get over one infection before another started. Recently he'd been tired all the time, so that things like football and cross-country runs at school had been quite beyond him. And the nose-bleeds had been a bit scary. Not scary in themselves, like colds they were something that several of his friends got from time to time, but they were such big ones. There was something so dramatic about the sight of blood pouring out everywhere, and the fact that they were so hard to stop. Perhaps it was a good thing that his mum had booked him in to see the doctor, maybe he needed some pills or something to get rid of whatever this thing was.

'Jamie Bevan for Dr Stagg,' said a disembodied voice through the intercom on the wall.

'That's us,' said his mum picking up her handbag. 'Are you ready? Don't forget your blazer.'

Dr Stagg turned out to be a motherly looking woman, quite young, not dressed in a white coat as Jamie had expected, but in a neat little red cardigan and a pair of grey checked trousers. She was sitting behind a computer, busily typing notes about her last patient.

Looking up she said, 'Hallo Jamie. Come and sit down. And you, Mrs Bevan, there's another chair over there. Now, what's the trouble?'

'Well, it started before Christmas—' began Clare, but Dr Stagg interrupted her.

'Let Jamie tell me,' she said smiling at him, 'after all, he's the one who's come to see me.'

Jamie told her all about the last two or three months and how he'd had one infection after another and had been feeling so tired, and how recently he'd been having so many nosebleeds. Dr Stagg listened carefully and wrote a couple of things on a pad of paper as he was speaking.

'It's probably just his age, isn't it?' said Clare when he had finished. 'He's grown so much in the last year.'

Dr Stagg put her pen down. 'We'll have to have a bit more of a look at him before we can say for certain. Could you hop up on the couch here for me, Jamie?'

She asked him to take his shirt off and spent the next few minutes examining him, listening to his chest with her stethoscope, taking his blood pressure and looking into his eyes and ears.

'Do you get breathless when you exercise?' she asked. 'Tired when you do anything active?'

Jamie considered. 'I do feel kind of droopy,' he admitted.

She patted his arm. 'OK. That's enough for now. I'll just put a few notes on your file while you get your shirt back on.'

She returned to her desk and typed at the computer keyboard for a few moments. By the time she had finished Jamie was back in the chair opposite her.

'So what do you think it is, doctor?' asked Clare.

'Hard to be sure. I think before we make any definite diagnosis we need to do some blood tests.' She scribbled something on the pad in front of her. 'If you take this down to reception they'll arrange for the nurse to take some blood from him.' She smiled at Jamie again who was looking distinctly alarmed. 'Don't worry, you'll hardly feel a thing, just a little prick.'

'What about school?' asked Clare. 'Should I keep him off?'

'No, not if he feels like going. Play it by ear. He seems a sensible young man, I'm sure he won't try it on. Will you, Jamie?'

'Course not,' he said indignantly, 'anyway I've got exams next term. I mustn't miss anything crucial.'

'Fine. Well, we'll be in touch as soon as the results of the blood test come back. In the meantime, take it easy as much as you can.'

Jamie and his mum returned to Reception and were directed to the practice nurse's room. There was another wait of about twenty minutes before the nurse was free to see them; this time they had to sit in a smaller room with several other people sitting on upright chairs against the wall.

'I wonder if it's glandular fever,' said Clare as they sat waiting, 'I remember Janey Briggs getting glandular fever a couple of years ago and she had to have blood tests like this. She was always tired too, just like you. It went on for ages – several months in fact. Perhaps that's what you've got.'

'I hope not,' said Jamie. There was no way he could afford to be ill for several months. Not just because of exams; he was hoping to be in the swimming team again in the summer and would need to do loads of training if he wanted to be considered.

At last the nurse was ready for them and Jamie had to roll his sleeve up for her to take blood. Dr Stagg had been right, it didn't really hurt, just as long as you looked the other way and didn't see the needle go in, but he couldn't resist watching with morbid fascination as his blood was sucked up into the syringe. It was hard to believe that the red liquid was actually coming out of his own vein and that a second ago it had been inside his arm. He watched as the nurse removed the needle, screwed a lid onto the sample and wrote out a label to stick on the side.

It was Wednesday night before the youth group were able to do any more work on the Halfway House. Ben rang several of them and arranged to meet them all there after school.

'But mind you leave time to do your homework,' he said to Gemma when he had told her what time to be there. Gemma was famous for doing her homework during registration on the morning it had to be handed in. Laura was always telling her off for this, but she might as well have talked to the wind for all the good it did. Laura herself always did homework on the day it was set in case something prevented her from doing it later.

'You're mad,' Gemma said to her on one such occasion, 'the world might come to an end before Thursday, and then you'd have wasted a whole hour of the last day of your life doing maths homework. Whereas I'd be out partying till the very last minute.'

'Ah yes,' put in Clicker who was listening to this conversation, 'but maybe only people who've done their homework are let into heaven. Have you thought of that?'

Gemma gave him a withering look. 'As if,' she said, in her most scathing voice.

Ben and Noah were the first to arrive that evening, Ben jangling the keys in his hand as they walked up the hill. As they neared the Halfway House Noah came to an abrupt halt and stared at the building.

'Look!' he exclaimed. 'Someone's graffiti'd all over the front!'

It was true. There, in black paint on the wall, was a cartoon figure of an angel busy at work with an electric drill. The angel was wearing overalls but wings sprouted from his shoulders and a halo rested on his hard hat. Underneath, in huge straggly letters, were sprayed the words

**RELIGUS NUTHOUSE. HOLY JOES ONLY
SINERS NEED NOT APPLY.**

There were several more messages painted on the door, suggesting in fairly colourful language what the inmates of the Halfway House might like to do with themselves. Noah was not a particularly good speller himself but it didn't take much intelligence to work out that the anonymous sprayer had had more practice at spelling obscenities than words like 'religious' and 'sinners'.

'Who could've done that?' he said, eyes wide with disbelief.

'I think I've a fairly good idea,' said his father grimly. 'But it'll be hard to prove. Come on, let's get in there and find something to clean it off. I think we've got some paint-stripper at the back which should do the trick.'

'Whoever did it is a cool artist,' observed Noah. 'Eat yer heart out, Rolf Harris.'

As Ben was unlocking the door, the rest of the helpers arrived. Laura had come up the hill with Clicker; she was not going out alone in the dark after last Saturday's encounter. There were several shocked exclamations as one after another saw the words daubed across the front of the building.

'Why would anyone have it in for us?' asked Gemma. 'You'd think they'd be pleased that we're making a place for people to go.'

Laura didn't reply. She, like Ben, had a pretty good idea who was responsible, and her heart sank at the thought that the boys who had caused her so much trouble on Saturday had obviously decided that the club should be their newest target for vandalism. There would be no stopping them once they got started.

'Ignore it,' she said, dumping her coat on the floor and starting to attack a new patch of wall. 'They're only trying to rile us. Load of losers, that's all they are.'

It wasn't so much fun working that evening as it had been on Saturday. For one thing, it was dark and the lighting in the pub was so subdued it was hard to see what they were doing properly. Then Noah had left his stereo at home so there was no music to sing along to. They were all feeling quite tired after a long day at school and were beginning to realise just how much work lay ahead of them before the club would be ready for use. There could be no short cuts, they would just have to keep at it till it was done.

'Cheer up, you guys,' said Ben after they had been working for about an hour. 'I've never known you all be so quiet. We'll only do another half-hour or so – I can see you're all knackered.' He glanced at Noah. 'Missing the water fights, eh, son?'

Noah attempted a smile. He did miss Jamie when he wasn't around; no one else was quite so ready for a bit of messing about. He was about to say something along those lines but was interrupted by the sound of shouting outside in the street. They all stopped talking in order to hear better.

'Ber-others and Sisters! I call on you to reee-pent!' someone was yelling.

'Al-lay-loooo-ya! Per-aise the Lee-ord!' came an instant response.

'Aay-men!' shouted a third voice.

'Bread of he-ea-ven, bread of he-ea-ven, feed me now and evermore-ore-ore-ore-ore...' sang another in a raucous tenor which suggested that the singer had gained his knowledge of hymns from the rugby pitch rather than from any kind of church.

Laura put down the scrubbing brush she was holding and climbed up on a chair to look out of the high window above the door. She had to peer into the darkness to see properly but could just make out the shapes of Lee, Vinny, Robbie

and a couple of others dancing about on the pavement, dou-
bled up with delight at their own cleverness, quite unaware
that she was watching them from above.

'It's them again,' she said to Ben. 'The blockheads
from Saturday.'

'Just pretend they're not there,' he said. 'They'll have
to get bored in the end.'

'Hey, preacher, do you save young girls?' came
another shout from outside. 'You do? Save me one for
Saturday night, wouldja?' Shrieks of laughter.

'You'll ne-e-ver walk a-lone!' carolled the hymn
singer who having exhausted his repertoire of rugby
songs had decided to move on to football chants.

There was a series of thuds as someone kicked the
door several times.

Ben sighed. 'You lot stay here,' he told the workers
as he crossed to the entrance. He opened the door and
peered into the night. Light flooded from the Halfway
House into the street and several figures moved back
into the safety of the shadows.

'Hallo lads, how are you? Do you want something?'

There was much jeering laughter at this.

'Mine's a pint of bitter and a packet of pork scratchings!' sniggered Vinny's voice from the darkness. 'It *is*
a pub, innit?' Then to Lee, 'Didja hear what I said, Lee?
A pint of bitter and a packet of pork scratchings!'

'Yeah, Vinny, I heard,' said Lee somewhat wearily.
'Sheer comic genius.'

'Well, you've had your laugh,' said Ben politely.
'Perhaps you'd like to leave us in peace now.'

'OK,' said Lee unexpectedly, 'come on lads, you
heard what Darkie said. Time to go home.'

From her position behind him Laura could see Ben
clenching his hands in rage at being called Darkie, but he
simply said, 'Good night then. Thanks for calling.'

There was more laughter at this but the group of youths seemed to be dispersing. Ben closed the door quietly and turned back into the pub. There was a pause as everyone inside heaved a sigh of relief.

But only for a moment. The silence was shattered by an almighty crash as a large stone hit the main bow window with huge force, sending several big pieces of jagged glass into the room, missing Clicker by inches and landing with a thud on the floor at his feet. More derisive laughter floated through the window, then the sound of running footsteps as the boys ran off into the night.

'Call the police, Ben,' said Fred, one of the assistant youth leaders who had come along to help. 'You can't let them get away with it. They'll only do it again.'

'Yes, go on Ben,' said Gemma, clearly shaken by what had happened.

'I guess I'll have to,' said Ben, but he looked uncertain. 'It's just that maybe they're the very kids who could get the most out of coming in here – I don't want to start a feud with them.'

'We don't want people like that,' said Gemma, 'they'll only ruin things. They'll smash the place up.'

'Yeah, but isn't that the whole point of the club?' pointed out Noah. 'To be a place where *anyone* can come and find people who'll accept them? Christian love and all that?'

'But there's got to be a limit,' objected Gemma. She was inclined to find Noah's inexhaustible supply of Christian love a bit trying.

'Ah, but has there?' said Ben.

Eventually it was agreed that Ben would ring the community policeman in the morning and ask him to keep a special eye on the club. In the meantime they stuffed newspaper into the smashed window to make the jagged edges as safe as possible, locked the building and went home. There was nothing there really worth nicking, said Ben, so they needn't worry too much about security.

For a few days work continued uninterrupted. Once the police were aware that there was a problem they made sure that one of their cars was in the area on Wednesday and Saturday nights, the two evenings when the youth group were in the Halfway House. For many of the young people it was beginning to become quite a regular social event, a good opportunity to meet up with mates.

Laura and Gemma saw each other most days anyway. They went to different schools, but their buses arrived at the same bus stop within five minutes of each other at the end of every day. Gemma's bus always got in first and except on the days when she had to baby-sit she usually waited for Laura's so they could walk home together. When Jamie wasn't ill he often accompanied them too, although he frequently had to stay late at school for team practices or play rehearsals.

On the Friday after Jamie's visit to the doctor Laura got off the bus alone, her school bag dangling from one shoulder.

'Hi,' she said to Gemma as she drew alongside her and they started to walk down the road.

'Hi yourself. No Jamie again?'

'Nope. Still off. He went to school on Wednesday and yesterday, but he was too tired again today.'

'Has he had the results of his blood test back?' To a suspicious mind Gemma's questions might have revealed a more than friendly interest in Jamie, but to Laura they seemed innocent enough.

'Yes, Dr Stagg rang yesterday. She wants him to go

to the hospital for more tests.'

'More tests? So do you think it *is* glandular fever?'

'Dunno. I think she would probably have said if it was. I don't really know much about it. Anyway, isn't glandular fever something you get by kissing?'

Gemma giggled. 'So what's he been up to, then, your brother?'

'Nothing as far as I know,' said Laura briskly, 'not that I'm my brother's keeper or anything. Do anything good today?'

'Not really. Had a French test, I did all right I suppose. Thirteen out of twenty. Loads of homework. Mum and Steve are going out at about eight o'clock to have a drink with some friends, so I've got to look after Jodie. But I don't really mind, *Top of the Pops* is on tonight.'

'Don't you ever get fed up with baby-sitting?' asked Laura. She occasionally sat for Noah's mum and dad when Noah wasn't able to and thought it was seriously hard work for the amount of money you got. But then there was a hideous number of children to look after in Noah's family. Six altogether including Noah.

'Doesn't bother me mostly,' said Gemma carelessly. 'Not unless it interferes with something I want to do.'

'Not even the nappies? You know, dirty ones and everything?'

'Used to it.' They were nearing Gemma's house. 'Look, do tell me when you hear anything more about Jamie, I'd like to be able to help or something if I can.'

'OK. Though if it is glandular fever, it's a bit late to do anything now. Apart from making sure you don't kiss him,' said Laura, cheerfully oblivious to the sudden colour flooding into Gemma's cheeks. 'See you.'

The following Monday Laura rang Gemma late in the

evening to tell her the news.

'Gemma, is that you?' she said, as soon as she answered and in a voice which immediately commanded Gemma's full attention.

'It's not glandular fever at all. It's leukaemia.'

4

'Mum, you're a nurse. What's leukaemia?'

Joanne, Gemma's mum, was downstairs in the kitchen washing up the last coffee cups of the day.

'It's an illness,' she replied, scrubbing at a particularly stubborn stain on one of the mugs. 'Something to do with the blood. Have you made your lunch for school tomorrow?'

'In a minute. Mum, what exactly is it?'

'What exactly is what? You'll find some cheese at the bottom of the fridge for your roll. Don't use it all, though, Steve'll want some for his sandwiches too. Oh, and I got some fresh apples today as you made such a fuss about the last lot. Though if you ask me the odd bruise never hurt anyone.'

'Mum,' said Gemma in exasperation. 'Leukaemia. What exactly is it?'

'It's a kind of cancer really,' said her mother, wiping down the kitchen counter as she spoke. 'You have these white blood cells – is this your biology homework? Shouldn't you be looking it up for yourself?'

'Just tell me.'

'Well, the white blood cells are supposed to repair themselves and reproduce all the time, but when you get leukaemia there are far too many white cells and they don't mature properly. Then because there are too many white cells they fill up your bone marrow and stop you from making red cells properly as well. You know about red cells and white cells? You have both in your blood and they do different things.'

'Yes, I think I remember learning about that,' said Gemma, trying to visualise the page in her biology textbook. 'And platelets.'

'That's right. And if your bone marrow isn't producing the right amount of normal cells you get into all sorts of trouble. You get anaemic if you haven't enough red cells, and if the white ones aren't working as they should you won't be properly protected against infections. And if you haven't the right amount of platelets you get bleeding in places like your gums, or from your nose.' She suddenly put down her J-cloth and stared at Gemma.

'Oh no,' she said. 'Not Jamie.'

Gemma nodded mutely.

Her mother sat down on a kitchen stool.

'Of course,' she said slowly, 'I should've... I mean, now you tell me I can see... Oh dear, poor Jamie.'

Gemma stood watching her. The next question was almost impossible to ask but she had to know the answer.

'Will he – you know – will he get better?'

Joanne rubbed absentmindedly at a spot on the kitchen table where the baby had left jammy finger marks and thought for a moment before answering.

'There's a very good chance he will. More and more people with leukaemia are being treated successfully these days and it helps that he's so young because the recovery rate is best in young people. But he's bound to have to go through some quite unpleasant treatment.'

'What sort of treatment?'

'Well, the aim is to destroy the leukaemia cells and get the bone marrow working properly again. That'll mean chemotherapy. They'll probably put a tube into one of his veins and then give him anti-cancer drugs through the tube. The side-effects aren't very nice, although by no means everyone gets all of them.'

'What are the side-effects?'

'Sickness. Extreme tiredness. Possibly a sore mouth. And his hair may fall out. But as I say, it doesn't happen to everyone.'

Gemma digested this information for a moment. 'Will he be off school for a long time?' she asked.

'It depends. He'll have to be off while he's actually having the chemotherapy, but he'll probably have it in doses over a few days at a time. I should think if he's feeling well enough in between he might be able to go to school, but he may not feel like it. Everyone reacts differently.' She looked at her daughter. 'Are you OK, Gem? You look really stunned.'

'Yeah, I'm all right,' said Gemma. 'Just a bit gobsmacked. Poor Jamie, though. What must he be feeling? And poor Laura.'

'Poor Jamie's mum and dad, too,' said Joanne, getting up from the table and going over to give Gemma a hug.

Nothing was quite what you expected, thought Jamie, as he lay in his hospital bed. Even the bed wasn't the usual sort you saw in medical dramas on telly, like *Casualty* or *ER*. It was an ordinary sort of bed like he had at home. His mother had gone down the corridor to make a cup of tea in the little kitchen they provided for patients' relatives, and he was enjoying a guilty moment of respite from her endless plumping of pillows and smoothing of duvets. Ever since the tall silver-haired consultant in Outpatients had explained what his illness was she'd clucked round him like a headless chicken, stroking his brow and feeding him nourishing drinks till he thought he'd go crazy.

Which was strange, when you came to think about it, because no one enjoyed being the main attraction as much as he did. He could remember having flu as a small boy, and the satisfying feeling of knowing that he would have his mother's full attention for several days, while Laura would just be left to get on with life as best she could. He had actually quite enjoyed being ill when it was something minor, it made him the star of the show for a few days. But this was something very different. For one thing, the tests had been no joke; all those needles and tubes, and all the bruises they left on his skin, besides which his mother's persistent fussing left him no space to think properly about what was happening. It was all deeply scary and he needed time to work out how he felt about everything. When the silver-haired doctor – Dr Rowlands was his name – had started talking to him about his illness and what it meant, he hadn't really been able to take it in. Phrases like 'usually recover' and 'outlook tends to be hopeful' and 'possible bone marrow transplant' floated in the air around his head but couldn't quite penetrate his brain. When he tried to focus on what people were saying to him, he just felt as if he was having a bad dream. Any minute now he would wake up and find life was normal again; he'd be going to school and going swimming and mucking about with Noah just as he'd always done, none of this would have really happened.

He hadn't seen any of his friends yet, apart from his dad and mum and Laura, of course. It had all happened too quickly for anyone at school or church to realise where he was, and now there would be no visitors till after the chemo. 'Chemo' was the short name for chemotherapy, he had discovered. He had learnt this from talking to other people on the ward, most of whom had been there for some time. There were four or five others there with him, quite a little community. All around his own age. Two of them were completely bald, he noticed; Dr Rowlands had said Jamie's own hair might fall out when he started treatment. He ran his hand through his spiky blond thatch and tried to imagine himself without it. It wouldn't be so bad, he thought; after all, David Beckham shaved his off and Posh still fancied him. Quite cool in fact. Perhaps he could grow it back in a Mohican.

He'd tried to talk to God, he knew that was what you were meant to do in a crisis, but whenever he did, all these black thoughts kept pouring into his head; all the what ifs and supposings, and he couldn't keep his mind on the job. It was hard to believe that God could help in anything as huge as this. But then Ben and Fred were always saying nothing was too hard for him. Maybe when Jamie had got his head together a bit more he'd ask his dad why it seemed as if God had gone away.

The Halfway House was ready for paint. All the walls had been stripped down to the plaster, the doors and skirting boards had been scrubbed and sanded to a point where the wood had almost been returned to its original state, and the mouldy old carpet had been pulled up leaving bare floorboards. The old curtains had gone, too, and a member of St Michael's who was a professional electrician had installed new lights, giving the building a completely different atmosphere.

There was some quite heated discussion over the colour scheme of the new club. Laura was all for painting it white, a colour, she pointed out, which would make the rooms look light and would go with any curtains or other furnishings they chose to put in there. Noah thought they should go for bold reds and blues, and Gemma was full of ideas about subtly tasteful colours with names like 'eau-de-nil' and 'crème de menthe' and 'café au lait'. Clicker had no opinion, he was simply waiting patiently for the day when the computers would be installed.

'If only Jamie could be here,' said Laura, as they sat in the club thumbing through DIY magazines. 'He has so many good ideas about this sort of thing.'

'There's nothing to stop you discussing it with him when you go to visit,' said Ben, 'I should think it would be good for him to have something other than his illness to talk about.'

'Oh, I don't think...' began Laura, then remembering how bored Jamie had looked when she had seen him last, she said 'well, p'raps you're right.'

'Take in a colour chart,' said Ben passing one to her.

'When can we come and see him?' Alan Sykes wanted to know. Alan was a good friend of Jamie's.

'He's having his first lot of chemo, but I'm sure you can visit him soon,' said Laura. 'He's not feeling bad at all. The doctor warned he might feel like puking, but so far he hasn't. I think it may take a while for the effects to build up.'

Alan pulled a face. 'Sounds nasty, just the same. Maybe I'll wait.'

This led to a rather unsavoury conversation about being sick and where everyone had done it and what colour it had been and why carrots always seemed to be involved. Laura sat quietly and listened, inwardly amazed at how callous her friends could be. Didn't they realise how serious Jamie's illness was?

Ben had to leave early that evening so he gave Fred the keys and left him to lock up with Noah and Clicker. The three of them lingered on in the street discussing the pool table and where the best place was to go to buy it.

'Oi!' called a voice. They looked up and there was Lee

coming down the hill, followed as usual by Vinny and two other bigger lads they hadn't seen before.

'That place finished yet?' Lee demanded.

'No,' replied Fred, 'it's still waiting to be painted. Why?'

'Jus' wondered,' he said. He was chewing a piece of gum and blew a large bubble.

One of the older boys spoke. 'Is it true, then, right, that anyone can come in here when it's finished? Like, anyone at all?'

'Well, you'd have to qualify age-wise,' said Fred guardedly, 'it's meant for school-age kids. And we wouldn't put up with antisocial behaviour or anyone messing the place up.'

'I getcher,' said the boy walking slowly round the front of the building and trying to peer through the windows. Ben had rigged up an old blanket to act as a blind so it was impossible to see in from the street. 'Nice tough windows, I see. Wouldn't break those in a hurry, I reckon.'

Vinny dug Lee in the ribs and smirked.

'Yeah, they're reinforced glass,' said Noah pointedly. 'You'd need a tank to break through those.'

Lee blew another bubble. 'How many rooms you got in there?'

'Two,' replied Fred, 'the main room and a games room. And a kitchen and toilets of course.'

'So is there another door?' asked the older boy. 'Somewhere at the back to put the rubbish out, that kinda thing?'

Noah started to reply but Fred interrupted. 'That's enough information for one day. If you want to come back and have a look when we're working in there, you're very welcome, but right now these guys need to get home. OK?'

'Yeah, come on, Lee, let's go. I'm starving. Let's go and get chips,' said Vinny, pulling at Lee's sleeve.

Lee glanced at the two older boys. The one who had done all the talking nodded almost imperceptibly and they carried on down the hill. Fred, Noah and Clicker watched them go.

'So what was that all about?' said Clicker.

'I don't know,' answered Fred, 'but I have a deeply bad feeling about those guys.'

Two weeks later Jamie was back at school. The day before he returned, Mrs Green, his form teacher, had spent some time talking to his class at Registration.

'We're hoping Jamie Bevan will be back tomorrow,' she told them, 'I think you all know he's been quite unwell and having treatment at Mulberry Grove Hospital. What you may not realise is that the drugs he's being given can have some unpleasant effects – they might make him look a bit different. I don't think he's been on the chemo long enough for that to have happened yet, but I'm telling you now so that you don't all pester him with lots of unnecessary questions; he's had enough to cope with without becoming a one-man side-show.'

She looked round to make sure everyone was listening.

'Hannah Barnes and Rachel Ericson, put away those pictures and try and concentrate on what I'm saying. What have I just been talking about?'

'Jamie Bevan, miss,' said Hannah, stuffing the photo of her latest pop idol under the desk. 'Miss, is it true he's gone bald?'

'Woss wrong with that?' growled Andy Walker from the back of the class, who wore his hair as short as he could get away with; there was a school rule about not actually shaving your head. A titter ran round the room.

'No, Hannah, he hasn't yet, but he has got to have a lot more treatment and it is quite likely that he may lose his hair temporarily. But it will grow back quickly, and in the meantime I'm sure he could do without a lot of comments.'

'Miss, miss, is he going to die?' asked Rachel, who enjoyed nothing more than a spot of drama.

'No, Rachel, he is not going to die. He's having these drugs so that he will get better. I just want you to be a bit thoughtful in the way that you treat him. Surely that's not so much to ask is it?'

'No, miss,' said Rachel, but she looked disappointed.

Noah was waiting for Jamie at his locker when he arrived at school. He had already visited him in hospital and was surprised to see how well and normal he looked now.

'Mrs Green talked to the class about you yesterday,' Noah said as they hung up their blazers, 'everyone knows about your illness.'

Jamie grimaced. 'Oh, great. So now I'm Exhibit A.'

There was an unusual hush as the two of them walked into the classroom.

'Hi, Jamie, how yah doing?' said one of the boys.

'Fine, thanks,' said Jamie shortly, making for his desk. Several people stood back to make way for him.

'Looks just the same to me,' murmured a girl with a nervous giggle.

'Sssh!' whispered another furiously. 'Have you forgotten what Mrs Green said?'

'I know. I was only trying to make him feel...'

'Well, don't, right.'

Jamie ignored this exchange and started getting books out of his bag. 'So what are we doing first?' he asked Noah who had sat down next to him. Amazing that he could have forgotten the timetable so quickly.

'Maths. Upstairs in Room 24. You haven't missed much, we've mostly been revising while you've been away.'

'Shall I help you carry your books up, Jamie?' asked Rachel Ericson, leaning up against the desk in front of him.

'I don't think that'll be necessary, thanks,' said Jamie.

'Buzz off, Rachel,' said Noah, 'he's all right, see?'

Last lesson of the morning was PE, usually one of Jamie's favourite lessons, but for the time being he was off games.

'You'd probably better go to the library and do some work,' suggested Mr Roberts, the PE teacher. 'I'm sure you've got loads to catch up with.'

On the way to the library he met Michelle Smith, a member of Encounter. Michelle was in Laura's year and hadn't seen him since he'd been ill.

'Hi, Michelle—' he started to say, but to his surprise she looked straight past him and rushed on down the corridor as if he didn't exist. He stared at her retreating back with puzzlement. Had he been gone so long that she hadn't recognised him?

By the end of the day he was exhausted. Laura was waiting for him at the school gate and seeing his pale face was full of concern.

'You look shattered,' she said. 'Dad'll have finished teaching his last lesson in half an hour, we could get a lift with him if you want, rather than lugging everything on the bus. How did your first day back go?'

'Don't ask. If it wasn't for Noah I wouldn't go back tomorrow. Half my class think I'm about to die and they've got to treat me like some kind of rare plant. The rest have decided I'm some kind of object of fascination who they can secretly stare at from behind their Bunsen burners whenever they think I'm not looking. Oh, and of course there's the ones who pretend I just don't exist at all,' he added remembering Michelle.

'No, really? Who was that?'

'Michelle Smith. She saw me coming down the passage and just avoided looking at me till she'd gone past.'

'What a weird thing to do. Perhaps she just didn't know what to say.'

'I can't think why not. Other people get ill, don't they? What's so special about me? Was it something Mrs Green said? If Dr Rowlands is right, I may well look really bizarre after the next dose. What'll they think then?'

'They'll get used to it,' said Laura. 'They'll have to, won't they? Just be patient, things'll get better.' She picked up her bag and slung it over her shoulder. 'What about all those photos you were going to do for Halfway House? Are you still going to do them?'

Jamie was relieved to have something else to talk about. 'Yes, I've got lots already, I put a whole load together while I was off school. I just want to get a few more of the hill. Now Spring's come I reckon I could get some really lovely shots of the area, specially down round the park. I just need to find a couple of people to be doing something in the pictures. I'm still hoping to get one of Noah running.'

'And Clicker clicking,' Laura reminded him.

'Yeah, only I'd like to take that actually in the club when the computers are in. Talking of which, when's that going to be?'

'Not till the painting's finished,' said his sister, 'but the colours you chose are going to look fantastic.'

At Jamie's suggestion they had finally settled on painting two walls of the main room a very deep dark blue, leaving the other two white. As he pointed out, the deep blue would make the room interesting and a bit mysterious, and the white would reflect the light and stop it from becoming too dark. The white would also provide a good backdrop for his photos. The table tennis room would be painted a light neutral sort of colour so that players would be able to see the ball easily. Most of the youth seemed satisfied with these choices although Gemma could still be heard muttering things about 'burnished amber' and 'crème framboise' quietly to herself.

'It's going to look great,' said Laura, 'I can hardly wait. Just stay well enough to get those photos done in time for the opening.'

'I'll do my best,' said Jamie.

5

Clicker was in a good mood. It was a Saturday morning in June, the sun was shining, his first two exams had gone well and today the computers were going to be installed at the Halfway House. It had been a long enough wait, what with having to get the painting finished first and then the hold-up in delivery from the computer warehouse. There were to be five machines, two specifically for games, and three for general use and surfing the net. A corner of the club had been specially turned into a computer area with tables set up next to each other for the monitors and keyboards, and there was a separate table at the end for a printer. Clicker had great plans for creating a Halfway House website with information on all the club's activities: Fred had offered his help, and he reckoned that together they could put together something really good.

Before going up to the club he had to go round to Jamie and Laura's house. Jamie had missed quite a bit of school over the last two months and Clicker had offered to lend him his biology revision guide before the exam. He hummed under his breath as he walked, busy with ideas about what he would include in the website. He wanted to have pages about all the regulars at the club, and then another section on the different events, so that if they had a table tennis or pool tournament he could keep an up-to-date record of who had won at each stage of the game and where people's names should be on the ladder.

Laura answered the door. 'Oh, it's you Clicker, come in. Jamie's at the back.'

She led the way through to the back room where the family usually watched telly. Jamie was sitting on the floor surrounded by photographs, scissors in hand.

'Come and have a look at this,' he said, holding out a picture without looking up.

Clicker sat down beside him and looked. It was a shot of Noah in his running vest, taken in black and white, and enlarged so that you could see the individual drops of sweat on his forehead. He was jogging across the park, long skinny dark legs contrasting sharply with white shorts, an expression of ferocious determination on his face. He was running across grass; in the background were trees and flowering shrubs, but they were blurry and out of focus so that your eye was immediately drawn to Noah's face. Determined to beat his own record, he clearly had more important things to think about than the sights and smells of the beautiful spring day. He was frowning with concentration, but you could still see the creases at the corners of his mouth where he usually smiled, and his dark eyes gleamed under the furrowed brows.

'Man. That is Noah!' said Clicker in admiration. 'Awesome. How did you get that?'

'It was easy,' said Jamie, 'you just gotta be there at the right moment. He always looks like that when he's running.'

'What else have you done?'

Jamie showed him more photos. There was Laura in jeans and sweatshirt polishing one of the tables in the club. There was Gemma, sitting in an armchair and reading a magazine, a half smile on her face as she turned the pages. There was Alan Sykes and Simon Menzies playing cards together. And there was a long thin sideways view of Ben, holding a sheaf of papers in one hand and pointing with the other.

'Ben giving orders,' grinned Clicker.

'Yeah, classic shot,' said Jamie proudly. He started to collect the pictures into a pile. 'All I'm missing now is you. Can I come and photograph you with the computers? Either today or tomorrow?'

'Course. But there should be one of you as well. Can't you get your dad to snap you somewhere?'

Jamie's face clouded over. 'Not right now, I look too weird. Maybe when my hair's come back.'

Clicker realised with a surprise that he had got so used to seeing Jamie with no hair over the last couple of months that he had almost forgotten what he used to look like. The first lot of chemo had had little effect on Jamie's appearance and straight afterwards he'd actually looked as if he was feeling much better. But soon after that he'd had to go back for several more doses, this time to destroy all the cancer cells that might be lurking unseen, and the higher doses of drugs had begun to have much more obvious consequences. Clicker knew Jamie had been very sick, finding it difficult to eat anything and even harder to keep it down; and then his hair had started falling out. It had come out in clumps so that there were still places left where it grew in wispy patches, but in the end it had annoyed him so much he'd got his mother to attack it with a razor.

'No one thinks about your hair now,' said Clicker, 'it just looks as though you've deliberately shaved it. Except for a few patches where you can see it's still growing.'

Laura frowned at him but what he said was true. You could see a kind of shadow where the last bits had been shaved, whereas where the hair had spontaneously fallen out Jamie's head was perfectly smooth and pink like a freshly boiled egg.

'Anyway, I still think you should have your photo up there with the rest,' Clicker went on. 'I mean, you are a kind of founder member, and everyone knows you.'

'Clicker, do you want to come in the kitchen and get a drink?' asked Laura suddenly, in her most commanding Come and Talk Somewhere Private voice.

He followed her into the kitchen.

'It's not just his hair,' she said in an undertone, pushing the door behind them and getting two glasses out of the cupboard. 'Haven't you noticed his face? How it's all puffy and strange?'

'Um, well yes, I s'pose I have. Is that because of the drugs too?'

'It's the steroids – he has to have them as well as the chemotherapy. He really hates the way he looks at the moment, so don't go on about it any more.'

Clicker was abashed. 'Sorry, I didn't realise.'

'Are you talking about me?' called Jamie from next door. 'I'd like a drink too if you're making one. Or are you too busy discussing how freaky I look?'

'Don't be stupid!' shouted Laura, quickly filling a third glass with juice. She put the three drinks on a tray and returned to the other room, followed by Clicker. Passing a glass to her brother she added, 'Don't you think we've got better things to talk about than you?'

The phone rang.

'Laura speaking. Yes… yes…' Her eyes widened. 'You're kidding. Not really. Just how cool is that?…Yes, he's here, and Clicker… yeah, I'll tell them. See you soon.' She replaced the handset.

'That was Ben. They've fixed a date for the official opening of the club – the first Saturday in July. And guess what – they've got Miranda Jukes to come and open it! Brilliant or what?'

'Wow,' said Jamie, 'Miranda Jukes off *Just Up Your Street*? How on earth did he manage that?'

'Apparently when she's not doing house makeover programmes she's really into helping community projects and stuff. When you think about it, Halfway House combines the two; we're a community project *and* a makeover.'

'Excellent,' said Jamie, 'P'raps we could get her to bring some TV cameras along and get us into the local news.'

'All in hand,' said Laura smugly, 'it's already planned. And the *Stanworth Advertiser*. We're going to be famous.'

Once the computers were installed, the Halfway House was almost finished. The youth group were justifiably proud of it. Even the outside looked new, the brickwork scrubbed clean and the door and window frames freshly painted. Jamie's dad was busy constructing a new sign to hang over the entrance where the pub sign used to be.

Graffiti continued to be a problem. Although not on the scale of the artwork spray-painted on the wall and door that first time, it was still common to arrive at the building after a Saturday night and find messages like 'Jade loves Matt' scratched on the door, or 'Kylie 4 Mick – to eternity and beyond' with a little heart engraved beneath it. Short of posting a twenty-four hour armed guard on the pavement there seemed to be no way of getting round this except to keep rubbing it down and painting it over.

Arriving at the club with his dad on Sunday afternoon, camera hanging over one arm and portfolio tucked under the other, Jamie stopped in the doorway and looked round in real admiration. It was two or three weeks since he'd felt well enough to go there, and the change in that time had been considerable.

'Knockout,' he breathed, gazing at the pool table which occupied pride of place in the middle of the room. The coloured balls shone red and yellow against the green surface, bright and glossy in the low-hanging overhead light.

He walked round, touching the little tables and chairs lightly as he passed, and pausing by the re-designed bar which now displayed rows of soft drinks and baskets containing bags of crisps. A coffee and tea machine stood behind the bar against the dark blue wall. Definitely a good choice of colour, thought Jamie with satisfaction.

Clive was watching for his reactions.

'Like it?' he asked.

'It's awesome,' said Jamie with feeling. 'And my pictures can go up here?' He pointed at the large blank white wall on the right of the bar.

'Yes, that's the spot we've reserved for you,' said his dad.

They had arranged to meet Clicker to take the last few photographs, but so far he hadn't turned up, so they sat down at one of the little tables, Jamie laying his camera and portfolio carefully in front of him.

'Did you mind missing so much of the building and painting?' asked his dad.

'It wasn't the best thing that ever happened to me,' said Jamie. 'None of this was. In fact, to be honest, the last six months have been nightmarish. I didn't know it was possible to feel so gross.'

'But you've done so well,' said Clive, 'and once you get over all this chemo you're going to be fine. Everything'll be OK again.'

Jamie looked at his dad sharply, trying to gauge if he was telling the truth.

'What if the chemo doesn't work?' he said slowly, 'or supposing I... what if it all comes back?' He hadn't dared put this question to anyone before; even the doctor had avoided talking about it, although Jamie knew it was a possibility.

'It won't,' said Clive, with some finality.

Jamie sat quietly for a moment. He had made a determined effort to blank all these sort of questions out of his mind, but suddenly it seemed very important to know exactly what his father thought.

'You know at the beginning when I was in hospital the first time?' he said. 'I tried to pray, you know, like you're supposed to, but then I kept thinking, supposing God doesn't really exist? What if it's all just a fairy story? Supposing it's just something adults tell you in Sunday school to make you behave? What would happen to me if I – you know, if it didn't all come right? Would I just stop existing? And anyway,' he added in a rush, 'even if God is real, I'm not sure if I really want to go to heaven. I think I'd rather stay here and muck about with Noah and the other guys, and take pictures and go swimming and all those things.'

His dad sighed. 'Jamie, man, I wish I could tell you all the answers. No one knows for sure, do they? If we did, it wouldn't be faith.'

'But you believe it. Why?'

'I guess because I've tried living it and it seems to make sense. If you try not to believe, that's even harder.'

'You say that, but hardly anyone does. No one at school ever thinks about God except Noah and maybe one or two others. Mostly people are only interested in sport and music and having a good time.'

'But perhaps that's because they've never been faced with anything difficult the way you're being now. I think nearly everyone starts praying when things go really wrong.'

'What, like soldiers on the battlefield and that sort of thing?'

'Yeah, kind of, but more obvious things than that. Even one of the other teachers at school told me they'd say a prayer for you when they knew you were ill, someone who doesn't usually have any time for religion.'

'Really?' said Jamie with interest. 'Who was that?'

'Your form teacher, as it happens. Which just goes to show that people do think there's someone out there and that it's worth trying to communicate sometimes.'

'But isn't that just wishful thinking? Trying to invent something to make them feel better?'

His dad tried another angle. 'Take this photography. You're getting really good, you know that? This last lot of pictures you've taken are the most interesting you've ever done, and you know why? It's because you've focused on the little details that give people their individuality. Like this one of Noah,' he picked up the photo. 'You can see his whole character here in his face, even though he's so young. And look at the muscles in his legs, each of them vital to his running skills. Then look at this one of Gemma, how different it is, and how every strand of her hair shows up. Those things never got there by chance, they're what makes Noah Noah and Gemma Gemma. Someone must've designed them. And if there's a creator, then he cares about his creation and it matters to him when things go wrong with it. That was the whole point of Jesus coming, wasn't it? To try to put things right in a spoilt world? I can't tell you why it should be you who has this gruesome thing to bear, but, man, I'm sure you haven't been left just to get on with it alone.'

'It doesn't seem very fair, though, does it,' said Jamie, his mind flitting to all the revision he hadn't been able to do for his exams and all the swimming he'd missed.

'No, it doesn't,' replied his dad. 'And I don't really know the answer to that. I wish I did.' His eyes looked unnaturally bright and for a moment Jamie was terribly afraid he was going to get emotional, but at that moment the door of the club was flung open and Clicker burst in. His hair was sticking up on end and there were splashes of wet mud clinging to his T-shirt.

'They're there again,' he managed to get out between gasps of breath. 'I saw Robbie on his own an' I was trying to tell him about the opening and everything, and how great it was going to be – but then Lee an' all them came and started throwing stuff at me and trying to trip me up. I had to run all the way up the hill.' He collapsed into the nearest chair and sat there, panting. His glasses had slipped sideways and taking them off, he started to polish them furiously on a clean patch of his shirt.

Jamie's dad strode to the door and looked out into the street. There was no sign of anyone, the road was silent with the unnatural quiet which always descended on the town on Sunday afternoons when all the shops were shut.

'They've gone now, you can relax,' he said to Clicker. 'Go and clean yourself up, I think Joanne put some soap in the wash-basins yesterday. You'll have to put Jamie's jumper over your shirt for the photos. Seems like we're going to have to try to sort this out once and for all.'

Only a few hundred yards away, in the park across the road, Lee, Robbie and Vinny had met up with Max and Dennis, the two older boys who had started hanging around with them in the last couple of months. They were lurking in their usual haunt, the gap between the back of the public toilets and a row of bushes, well concealed from casual passers-by.

'Well?' said Max, the tallest, rolling some evil looking tobacco into a slip of paper as he spoke. 'How are our little Christians?'

Lee grinned. 'Busy little bees, ain't they, Robbie? Robbie here had quite a chat with the geeky feller in the specs.'

Max lit up, blew out a puff of smoke and passed the joint to Dennis for a drag. 'Friendsa yours, are they Robbie? Gonna join the club are yer?'

Robbie gave an unsteady laugh. 'Course not. He was just telling me about the opening day. They've got Miranda Jukes coming to cut the ribbon and make speeches.'

Max raised an eyebrow. 'Miranda Jukes, eh? Impressive. When's that then?'

'July 4th. They're having a big service thing and I think the mayor's coming too, and, like, a mega party in the club.'

'Are they indeed? A party. Well, I never. I thought those guys didn't approve of parties. I wonder…'

'Wotcher thinkin', Max?' said Dennis.

'I was thinking… maybe we could make our contribution to the community effort, eh lads?'

'Like how?' asked Lee dubiously.

'Like, why don't we see if we can hot things up a bit? Give them a day to remember, that kind of thing.'

'I'm not doing anything illegal,' said Robbie anxiously. 'If you're going against the law you can count me out.'

'Oh yeah, I was forgetting, you're mates with all those mingin' little hymn-singers. Which is strange, 'cause wasn't you one of the stone-chuckers?'

Robbie looked troubled. 'I didn't actually throw one, that was Lee and Vinny. Look, I gotta go home now.' He picked his jacket off the grass.

'Back to Mummy, little boy?' sneered Max. 'Don't like the nasty big bad men? Off you go then, but—' he grabbed Robbie's shirtfront and pulled him up so they were eyeball to eyeball, '—no telling tales. Not to anyone. Not if you don't want the law breathing down your neck. Right?'

Robbie blinked at him, then extricated himself, turned and ran off.

'So what's the plan, then, Maxie?' asked Dennis.

'Haven't worked out the details yet,' said Max, rubbing his chin reflectively. 'Let's just say, this could be the hottest party in town.'

6

Gemma had spent all her hard-earned baby-sitting money on a new outfit in honour of Miranda Jukes and the opening ceremony; a dead slinky skirt and a little strappy top which showed her midriff. After all, if there was a chance of getting her picture in the papers, or better still on the telly, she certainly wasn't going to be caught in some old T-shirt out of the dark ages. She decided she needed to do something with her hair as well, and managed to cajole her mum's hairdresser friend Paula into having a go at it after school on Friday night. After some discussion she settled on braids, a long and tedious operation, but definitely worth the hassle.

Laura had sat beside her at Paula's kitchen table to watch the whole procedure and when it was finished looked critically at her friend's reflection in the mirror.

'Yes, not bad I suppose. Although you really need hair extensions for the full effect. What will you do when you want to wash it?'

'Who cares?' said Gemma. 'As long as it looks good tomorrow. Just think, there might even be a TV producer there – looking for star quality or something. I have to be ready.'

'It's only *local* telly, durr-brain. Local news, that's all it is. We'll probably only be on for about ten seconds, you know, the "and finally" slot. Anyway it's Miranda Jukes they'll be filming, not you.'

Gemma pouted. 'You never know. I might just catch someone's eye. You should wear something special too,' she added, looking severely at Laura's bedraggled school shirt and wispy hair dragged back into a scrunchy.

She thanked Paula and the two girls meandered down the road towards their homes. As they passed the Halfway House Laura stood on tiptoe and peered through the window.

'No one there. It's all ready, though. Looks dead nice. Streamers and balloons and everything.'

'Hope it's well locked up,' said Gemma, 'if those blokes got in...'

'It'll be fine.' They walked on down the hill.

'Jamie's photos look really brilliant,' said Laura, 'I just wish there was one of him. He's so bloomin' touchy about everything these days. Shouts at you if you even look at him.'

'He does look a bit different, though, doesn't he?' observed Gemma. If the truth be told, she had been quite taken aback by the change in Jamie's appearance; it was hard to remember the blond, sporty looking bloke he used to be.

'Yes, but there's no need for him to be quite so ratty. He can be a real pain at times,' said Laura.

'He *will* come tomorrow, won't he? I hope he's not going to suddenly drop out at the last minute or anything.'

'Who knows?' replied Laura. 'He's just finished another lot of chemo so he's very tired at the moment. He was really sick this time as well. It gets me down, you know Gem, we can't do anything like we used to 'cause we've always got to take him into consideration.

We haven't even been to stay with Gran for weeks and you know how we usually go there pretty well every couple of months. And Mum and Dad spend all their time worrying about him. Sometimes I don't think they'd even notice if I moved out.'

Gemma was shocked. 'Don't talk like that, Laura, you mustn't. You know he can't help being ill.'

'Yes, I know,' sighed Laura, 'but it's gone on for over six months now and I'd like my life back. It was bad enough having a brother who was so much cleverer and sportier than me, but to have one who's ill all the time is just the pits. I can't even have a decent argument with him without Mum telling me not to upset him. No one seems to care that *I* might be upset too. All the things we normally do have gone right out of the window, 'specially with Mum and Dad taking it in turns to have time off from work and being around the house all the time.'

Gemma was silent. She had no idea what to say, the whole situation was completely out of her experience. She had some sort of feeling that Laura ought to try harder to make allowances, but she could see how difficult it must be.

'It must be tough,' she said. She added awkwardly, 'Look, you know, I'm always here if you need someone to talk to…'

'Thanks,' said Laura, flashing her a quick smile. 'Anyway, let's hope he does come tomorrow. It'd do him good to be with all his mates.'

Although she didn't tell Gemma, she was particularly worried about Jamie just at present; he had been really unwell for the last couple of days. Usually she could get some spark of interest out of him when she talked about what had been going on at school but yesterday all he had wanted to do was sleep.

It was three o'clock in the morning and Ben was having a nightmare. In his dream it was the next day, the afternoon of the club's opening, and he and Miranda Jukes were having an argument.

'I can't possibly open this building till you do something about the unspeakably dreadful colours,' Miranda was saying. 'Just look at it – no one's touched it for years!' She was wearing a vast black hat and carried a great big hold-all over one arm.

Looking around at the decor Ben saw that it was indeed hideous: orange and lime green floral wallpaper, and a sort of browny coloured mould creeping over the ceiling.

'I'll have to bring in my makeover team,' said Miranda, 'it's going to take about a week. Can you wait that long?'

'But we were hoping you would open it today,' said Ben desperately, 'couldn't you just open it anyway and we'll promise to re-decorate later?'

'Nonsense!' said Miranda briskly, extracting an outsize mobile phone from her huge shoulder bag. 'I'll ring the team and get them to come over now!'

The phone rang shrilly, over and over again in the darkened room.

'What...?' mumbled Ben, drugged with sleep and still half in his dream. He reached a hand out from under the duvet and swiped at the phone, sending it flying to the floor. Muttering under his breath he leaned over the side of the bed and scooped it to his ear.

'Huh?' No one seemed to be there.

'Have you got it the right way up?' asked a drowsy voice from the other side of the bed. His wife Sue was much better at waking up quickly than he was.

'What? Oh, yeah, right, see what you mean.' He turned the receiver round and spoke into the mouthpiece, 'Ben Richardson.'

An official sounding voice came over the line. 'Mr Richardson. So sorry to disturb you at this time of night but I thought we'd better let you know. This is Sergeant Grey from Stanworth Police Station. I believe you're the key-holder for the Halfway House on Devonshire Hill? And you're responsible for the improvements that have been going on there recently?'

Ben sat up in bed. 'That's right. Has something happened?'

'I'm sorry to have to tell you this but there's been a fire in the building.'

'A fire? What do you mean? A fire in the Halfway House?'

'That's right, sir. It must have been burning some time before the alarm was raised as it seems to have done quite a lot of damage.'

Ben swung his legs over the side of the bed, fumbling for his clothes as he talked.

'What kind of damage?'

'Well, it seems to have started at the back, sir. Round the service area. As far as we can see most of the kitchen has been affected and the smaller room at the side. We can't get in there yet as it's still quite dangerous, but I think the fire brigade have got it pretty much under control.'

'I'm coming down,' said Ben, reaching for his shoes. 'I'll be right there.'

'There's not much you can do at the moment, sir, not until the fire is completely out. But of course, I understand that you want to be there immediately. And with your knowledge of the building perhaps we can get some idea of how it started.'

'OK. I'm on my way. Thanks for letting me know.'

'That's all right, sir, that's what we're here for. In fact we've had quite a busy night tonight, several petty thefts and a car or two missing, joy-riders probably. And there was a break-in at St Michael's church earlier in the evening as well.'

'You're kidding.'

'Not a word of a lie. Funny business, nothing valuable missing – not like you might expect with kids wanting money for alcohol or drugs – I could understand that.'

'So what did they take?'

'Hymnbooks and Bibles, sir. All the books they could lay hands on. The whole lot gone. What on earth could they have wanted them for? Beats me.'

By ten o'clock the next morning the word had got round and most of Encounter and several of their parents were to be found standing on the pavement outside the Halfway House gazing with disbelief at the blackened building. Two of the side windows had cracked in the heat and smoke still wafted out, thick and foul-smelling, making some of the watching crowd cough.

The worst of the damage was at the back. Firemen who had been into the building said they reckoned it had begun in the kitchen area and spread sideways, burning out the table tennis room and all the equipment in it, and then going on to destroy everything against one wall of the main room. Two-thirds of the main room had escaped reasonably unscathed and it seemed to be smoke rather than flames that had had the worst effect.

'How could it have happened?' wailed Michelle Smith to Clicker as she and Gemma stood amongst the little gathering.

'S'obvious, isn't it?' he said. 'I should've thought anyone would know.'

'Know what?'

'Arson, dummy,' said Clicker. 'Someone did it on purpose.'

Michelle looked at him with big eyes. 'You mean someone deliberately set fire to it, knowing it was the opening day today? What a dreadful thing to say. Who would do a thing like that?'

'Lee and friends, course, stupid. Who else?' Clicker spoke rather more sharply than usual; he was suffering from a slightly guilty conscience from passing on so much information about the opening to Robbie.

'How do you know?' asked Gemma.

'It must be. They've been bugging us ever since we started work here. First the shouting, then the graffiti, then the stones and now this. Who else could it be?'

'But can it be proved?' said Alan Sykes who was listening to this conversation. 'You can't just make accusations without proof.'

'Easy,' said Clicker. 'You just gotta find out exactly where the fire began, then you're bound to find clues which link up to them. Fingerprints or something.'

'But won't that all have been destroyed by the fire?' asked Michelle.

'I don't know, I'm not a detective,' said Clicker patiently. 'But they must have ways. Hey—' he addressed a passing firefighter who had just come out of the building and was walking back to his fire engine, 'do they know what started the fire in there?'

'Books of some kind,' said the firefighter, 'they were stacked in a pile against the kitchen door and then someone set light to them. They'd all been soaked in petrol first – no doubt at all that someone did it on purpose.'

'See?' said Clicker jubilantly. 'What did I tell you? I bet if you go to Lee's house now you'd find something that'd give him away, petrol on his clothes or an old can or something. Criminals never completely cover their tracks.'

'I wonder what Ben's going to do,' said Michelle, 'Miranda Jukes is due this afternoon at two o'clock. I suppose they'll have to put her off.'

'They can't do that,' said Gemma, 'she'll be on her way here already. What on earth will he tell her?'

A squeal of brakes heralded the arrival of Ben's ancient van as he pulled up in front of them. He had spent most of the night with the police outside the club answering questions, and had just been back to his house to shower, have breakfast and make a few phone-calls.

He leaned out of the window and called to them. 'You people want to come back to our place? I'd better tell you what's going on; we've had to change a whole lot of things. I'm going back there in the van now – if you walk down, I'll get Sue to put the kettle on.'

Within half an hour about a dozen of them were crowding into the Richardsons' kitchen and Noah's mum was handing round tea and squash.

Ben perched on a stool at the head of the table and took a gulp of tea. 'Right, folks. Here's the deal. The fire must have started around midnight, initially set off by someone who had previously broken into St Mike's, stolen all the books he could find in the church, heaped them against the wooden door at the back of the club, doused them in petrol and chucked a lighted match at them.' He grinned ruefully. 'Must've been someone with a deeply ironic sense of humour. Anyway, there's no way we can go ahead with the opening today, so I've rung all the main guests like the mayor and the guy who was coming to represent the bishop, and of course, our friend Miranda—' there was a general mur-mur of disappointment at this '—yes, I know, it's a real shame, but what can we do? Apart from those people who were going to have to make a special journey, everyone else is fairly local and I suspect the word will get round very quickly about what's happened. We'll have to wait until the damage has been properly assessed before we can estimate how long it's going to take to put it all right again. Then we can fix another opening date.'

There were a few groans of protest, and Laura said, 'You mean we've got to start work all over again? All the painting and wiring and everything? All that time we spent wasted?'

''Fraid so,' said Ben. 'Believe me, no one is more gutted than me. But let's not panic yet, we still don't know how bad it is. At least we were well covered by insurance, so we're not going to be out of pocket.'

'I'm blowed if I'm going to give up any more time wearing myself out and getting filthy after school,' muttered one disgruntled voice in an undertone, and another added, ''Specially if it's just gonna be burnt down again. We all know who did it, after all.'

'Which brings me to my next point,' interjected Ben. 'I know you're all thinking you know who was responsible for the fire, and I have to admit that to begin with I had the same thought, so I gave a couple of names to the police. However, when the police went round to visit the boys in question, Lee Francis, Robbie King and Vincent Parker, it turned out that none of them could possibly have been anywhere near the area last night because all of them were at Honeypot, the club over in Trigton. Dozens of people saw them there and can vouch for the fact that they were there all evening and stayed on into the early hours, well after the time when the fire started. In fact when the police interviewed them they seemed genuinely surprised at what had happened.'

'Yeah, right,' said Clicker disbelievingly. 'Like they'd say, "Oh, yes, officer, we thought this was going to happen. Shall we show you how we did it?"'

'But you can't dispute their alibi,' pointed out Sophie Illingworth.

'Well if it wasn't them, it must have been friends of theirs. What about those other guys they kicked around with – Max, wasn't it, and Dennis?'

'They are a possibility,' agreed Ben, 'and in fact the police tried to find them but it seems they have disappeared.'

'There you are! Case solved,' said Clicker triumphantly. 'They would've known we'd be on to them before long, so obviously they've done a bunk.'

'Well, whatever actually happened, there's one interesting thing about this,' said Ben. 'Because the fire was at the back of the building it could have got much worse before anyone noticed it. It was the early hours of the morning, remember, no one around, and you'd have to go down the alleyway behind the shops to see anything. But the reason the fire brigade got onto it so quickly was because someone rang up and warned them there might be trouble. So someone knew about the fire before it happened. If it hadn't been for that there might be no building left there at all today.'

There was a ring at the door and Sue went to answer it. Returning a couple of minutes later she said to Laura, 'Your dad's out here, he wants you to go home. He's got the car with him.'

Laura looked puzzled. 'Why would he bring the car? It's only five minutes walk back to our house. Oh well, I suppose I'd better go. I'm surprised he hasn't been here this morning; I'd've thought he'd be the first person to rush up after all the work he's done on the club. But he was busy fussing round Jamie when I left, so p'raps he felt he couldn't.' She shrugged her shoulders and walked to the door. 'Bye, everyone.'

'Bye, Laura,' said several voices in unison.

As the door closed behind her, Clicker suddenly had a thought.

'Ben,' he said urgently, 'what happened to Jamie's photos?'

'All ruined, I'm afraid,' replied Ben. 'Every single one of them. Some of them actually burned, and others were destroyed by the smoke. But it's not the end of the world, I assume he's still got the negatives tucked away somewhere.'

'Wrong,' said Alan Sykes. 'I know for a fact he took the negatives into the club and left them on the shelf in the kitchen area. He was hoping to pass them on to the *Stanworth Advertiser* chappie in the hopes they might be used in the report. They must have gone up in smoke with everything else.'

Gemma, who up until now had been unnaturally silent, suddenly burst out, 'It's just so *unfair*! The whole thing! After all the effort we've put in and all the money that's been raised and everything! And I even did my hair specially! I'd like to get my hands on the rotten losers who did this and knock the—'

'All right, Gemma, I think we all know what you'd like to knock out of them,' said Ben hastily. 'It *is* a bummer. But we're not going to let ourselves be defeated are we? Remember how excited we all were at the beginning? I'm still sure this is a special thing God wants us to do, and yeah, this may be a hiccup, but it's through hiccups that we grow. That's how we learn. Isn't it? Guys?'

He looked round the table at the sea of glum faces. Even Noah looked depressed.

'OK,' said Ben, 'end of sermon. Go home, all of you.

I'll contact you all in the next day or so when I have a clearer picture of how much work there is to do.'

They filed out in silence. 'Hope the opening day won't be postponed too far into the future,' muttered Gemma to Michelle as they left. 'My new outfit is strictly summer gear.'

7

'What's going on?' asked Laura as she and her father got into the car. 'Where are we going? Has something happened?'

'I've just got back from the hospital,' he said briefly, 'I'm afraid Jamie's not at all well. I've left him there with Mum and I'm going back as quickly as possible, but I've come home to get his things and to sort out something for you.'

Something in his voice sent an unexpected deep chill of fear right through her. He started the car and Laura noticed that his hands were trembling slightly on the steering wheel.

'But I thought he was getting better. I thought the chemo was working,' she said. 'What's wrong with him? Why is he ill again?'

Clive concentrated on pulling out into the road before speaking. 'It seems that the chemo can cause other complications. Because the treatment has destroyed all his white blood cells Jamie is much more open to infection than you or me. That's what he seems to have now, an infection which has given him an extremely high temperature and made him very ill indeed.'

Laura looked out of the car window at the familiar street which she walked down every day on her way home from school.

'So what will happen? They'll give him something to make it better, won't they?'

Her dad said nothing for a few moments but drove in silence till they reached their house. He switched off the engine and turned to face her.

'Laura. I have to tell you. We have to be prepared.' He looked down at his hands for a moment, clenching and unclenching his fists on his lap, and to her horror when he looked up again his cheeks were wet. 'It seems there's a chance he might not make it.'

Laura sat very still. 'What do you mean, not make it?'

'They'll give him antibiotics and all that. They'll try all they can. But it may be... it may be... that it won't be enough...' His voice faltered.

She struggled to take it in. 'But of course he'll get better. Dad, this is *Jamie* we're talking about. That sort of thing doesn't happen to Jamie.'

Jamie, the golden boy. Jamie, the swimming star. Jamie, the success story. Jamie, apple of his dad's eye. A tear had dripped onto her father's beard and hung there like a raindrop. Laura stared at it, dumbstruck. She didn't think she'd ever seen him cry before.

She tried to think about now, about what she must do.

'Look, don't worry about me. I'll go over to Gemma's. How long are you going to be at the hospital?'

'I don't know. It depends on what...'

'OK,' she said quickly, 'I'll get my toothbrush and PJs and go over there. Then if you need to stay the night with Jamie it'll be all right.'

He gave her a watery smile. 'That's what I hoped you'd do. We'll ring Gemma's mum in a minute and if she's happy with that arrangement I'll drop you up there on the way. I'll give you the ward number so you can contact me anytime.'

She nodded. 'What about visiting? Can I go and see him?'

'I don't know. We'll see what the doctors say. He's got such a fever, he's all muddled in his head – he might not know who you are. Perhaps we should wait a bit.'

'Fine,' she said, although she felt anything but fine. Somehow their roles seemed to have been reversed so that she was the parent and he was the child. She wondered how her capable, efficient mum would be coping up at the hospital.

They let themselves in to the silent empty house, and after phoning Joanne started to put together what they would need for the next twenty-four hours.

Laura sat on her bed and stuffed the T-shirt and shorts she wore in bed into her rucksack. What else should she take? What do you need when your brother might be dying? Her old ragged teddy bear who lived on her duvet was looking up at her beseechingly. OK Ted, in you go. What about her alarm clock? But presumably Gemma had one and could wake her up. She very much doubted she would sleep that well anyway.

Her eye fell upon her bedside table and the little Bible which her godmother had given her last Christmas. Strange that her dad hadn't even mentioned prayer; surely if ever they had needed God, now was the moment. She sat very still on the bed, hugging her pillow, and tried to focus her whole mind on talking to him.

Please God make Jamie be all right. I don't know what Dad would do without him. Don't let him die.

She tried to think about how it would be if her brother died but she found she couldn't picture it. The whole idea was just too difficult to imagine. He had always been there ever since she could remember, even before they had moved to Stanworth when she was four and he was five. Sometimes they fought, often he was wildly irritating, but up until now she had completely taken for granted that he was a normal part of her life which would never change.

Gemma was still at Ben's with the rest of Encounter when Laura's dad rang to arrange for Laura to come and stay, but when she got back at lunch-time Joanne told her what had happened. Gemma had come home completely preoccupied with gossip about the fire, but this latest piece of news banished all thoughts of the Halfway House from her head.

'How truly terrible,' she said, trying to imagine how Laura must be feeling. 'What can we do?'

'I've put the sofa bed in your room,' said her mum, 'but I'll need you to go to the shops for me later. I've only bought enough food for us three and the baby this evening and I'll need to get some more for Laura. If I give you a list will you both go and do a bit of shopping this afternoon? P'raps you could take Jodie with you too to give her a breath of fresh air?'

'Of course,' said Gemma, 'only won't Laura think it's a bit, you know, heartless being made to go shopping when Jamie is so ill?'

'We've still got to eat,' said her mum, 'anyway what do you expect her to do? Sit around all afternoon moping and waiting for her parents to ring? It'll be good for her to get out and do something.'

Joanne was right. When Laura arrived at their house she was very grateful to have something specific to do with Gemma. They fastened Jodie into her pushchair and set off to the shops. It was an extremely hot day and there was little shade along their route. As they walked, Jodie grizzled and tried to wriggle out of her straps; her little face was beetroot coloured and her curly brown hair stuck damply to her forehead. It was a relief to get into the cool supermarket, and after they'd completed their shopping they treated themselves to an ice cream each.

'Why don't we go back the other way?' said Gemma. 'Down the hill past the park. I know it's a longer way round, but there are more trees along there.'

'Yeah, whatever,' replied Laura. She sounded as if she was only half listening, as if it was hard to think about anything but Jamie.

They walked down the hill, along the edge of the park, enjoying the shade of the big horse chestnut trees which hung over the pavement. Laura pushed the buggy with one hand, while Gemma gave her full concentration to eating her ice cream. She had a special way of eating ice creams: first you licked the top into a perfect mound, then you flattened it with your tongue pushing it as far down into the cone as possible. After that you had to nibble the bottom of the cone to get rid of the boring bit where the ice cream hadn't reached. This left a hole in the bottom so you had to eat the rest very quickly before it all started to melt and drip through onto your clothes.

She was just at the licking-ice-cream-through-the-hole stage when she caught sight of Ben on the other side of the road, walking up the hill towards the Halfway House. There was a woman with him, a woman she hadn't seen before. The woman was tall and slim, she had short blonde hair and was dressed in a smart little white skirt and a pink top. She was wearing large sunglasses and a white jacket was slung over one shoulder. There was something very familiar about her...

'Miranda Jukes!' squawked Gemma, clutching so hard at Laura that she nearly let go of the buggy, sending it flying down the hill.

'What?'

'Look! Over there with Ben! Going into the club!'

Laura secured the brake on the pushchair and looked. It was indeed Miranda Jukes. Ignoring the large keep-out notices which covered the blackened entrance of the club, Ben unlocked the door and they both went in, unaware that they were being watched from the other side of the road.

'She came after all, then,' said Laura.

'I knew it!' exclaimed Gemma smugly. 'I told Michelle and Clicker it was too late to stop her coming for the opening. She had to come all the way from London, don't forget. Even if Ben rang her on the way it would've been too late to turn back.'

'Yes, but what's she doing in there now?' asked Laura, squatting down to dab ineffectively at the ice cream smeared all over Jodie's plump cheeks.

'No idea. P'raps she's just gone to look at the damage.' Gemma squinted at the closed door of the building. 'D'you think we could go in and talk to her? You know, just say we were passing kind of thing and thought we'd drop by, and oh, Ben, sorry, didn't realise you had a visitor…'

'No,' said Laura firmly. 'If she's there for a reason Ben'll tell us later. Come on, we ought to get back. Your mum will be worrying about Jodie. We've taken far too long already as it is.' She let the brake off the buggy and began to walk downhill again. Gemma dawdled behind her, frequently looking back to see if anything interesting was going on in the club.

As she had expected Laura slept badly that night. Her mum had rung during the evening to report on Jamie's progress and had been very subdued.

'I wish I could say he's out of the woods, but that wouldn't be true,' she'd said. Her voice sounded strange and muffled, not at all like her normal brisk cheery tones. 'He's awake at the moment but very weak from the fever, and although they're giving him every antibiotic under the sun to fight the infection, nothing really seems to be working.'

Laura had been at a loss to know how to reply. She longed to give her mum a big hug.

'Can I come and see him tomorrow?' she had asked eventually.

'Yes, I don't see why not. You'll have to wear a special gown, though, they are doing everything they can to keep the place germ-free.'

Sunday morning dawned, cloudless as Saturday, promising another scorching day. Laura had a headache when she woke, partly from being too hot and partly from tossing all night on unfamiliar lumps in her mattress. The sofa bed was hard and took up nearly all the available floor space in Gemma's room so that they had to climb round each other to get dressed.

At ten o'clock Laura's dad arrived to take her to the hospital. He looked pale and tired, and was very quiet as they drove. They parked in the large hospital car park and took the lift up to the third floor. They had to go through double doors into the ward and Jamie's room was almost immediately on the right. He had a side ward to himself and there was a large notice on the door saying BARRIER NURSING, NO ENTRY WITHOUT PROTECTIVE CLOTHING.

'We have to go and ask the nurse if we can go in,' said Laura's dad. 'She'll give us special things to wear to minimise the risk of germs.'

They found a nurse in the office across the corridor who gave them each a gown and cap and gloves to wear, and a mask to go over their faces. Laura, only able to see her dad's eyes, had a momentary desire to turn and run away. But her dad was already opening the door into Jamie's room.

Jamie seemed to be asleep. He lay still under the covers, breathing quietly. His face was very white and a tube ran from his hand to a plastic bag behind the end of the bed. A nurse was on one side of the bed, taking his pulse, and on the other side sat their mum stroking his fingers. She looked up as they came in, her eyes crinkled up above her mask as if she was pleased to see them. It was weird not being able to see her whole face.

'How is he?' asked their dad, quietly.

'He's sleeping,' said the nurse, answering for Clare. 'He's very peaceful at the moment, as you can see.'

'Come closer if you like, Laura,' said her mum.

Laura went a little closer to the bed. Her head was throbbing as if it would explode, the room felt stiflingly hot and the mask was stopping her from breathing properly. If only Jamie would open his eyes and smile at her.

Clare pulled a long stool out from under the bed, motioning for Laura to sit beside her. Laura sat quietly, gazing at her brother's pallid face while her parents talked to each other in undertones. There was nothing to do but sit: she felt awkward and in the way, as if she shouldn't be there.

After a few interminable minutes she said in a strained voice, 'I have to go. Dad, can you take me back?'

'But you've only just—'

'Take her, Clive,' said her mum. 'It probably wasn't a good idea after all.' She held her other hand out to Laura. 'Are you all right with Gemma, sweetheart? I know it's hard, but I don't know what else to suggest for you. We could get Grandma up, but she's so frail herself, I think it might be too much for her.'

'I'll be OK,' said Laura. She just wanted to leave the room as quickly as possible.

She leaned over Jamie's bed for a moment looking for some response in his white face.

'Jamie,' she whispered, 'it's me, Laura. Can you hear me? We're all thinking of you, Noah and Clicker and the rest of the gang. They're all going to get together at Ben's this morning just to pray for you. Even Gemma got up early specially to be there. So you see, you've got to get better.'

He slept peacefully, the faintest smile on his lips, as if he was enjoying a particularly good dream.

She put a hand on his arm.

'Bye, Jamie. See you soon.'

She gave her mum a quick kiss then hurried out into the corridor, followed by her dad. She had a desperate need to be with her friends, playing some of her favourite CDs with the rest of the gang, somewhere away from this antiseptic smell and the bleeping machines and subdued voices.

In the middle of the night there was a terrific thunderstorm. Laura, sleeping lightly, was woken by the first massive crash of thunder and sat bolt upright in bed. Gemma was already awake.

'Did you hear that?' she asked unnecessarily.

'Course I did,' said Laura, 'I'm not deaf. Sounded like the end of the world.'

'Are you frightened?'

'Nah. Not really. Only kids are frightened by thunderstorms.'

'Yeah, you're right,' said Gemma, sounding unconvinced.

'When we were little we both used to climb into bed with Dad and Mum when there was a storm,' said Laura, 'and Mum made up stories about God mowing his lawn or moving furniture. And when we got older she started telling us the scientific explanation for thunder and lightning. It's all to do with electricity being discharged between rain clouds. Actually I don't think she really understood it herself but it stops you being frightened when you realise it's not actually a giant walking across the roof of your house. You can face almost anything when you know the reason behind it.'

A brilliant flash lit up the room, followed almost immediately by another violent crash of thunder. Gemma giggled nervously. 'Are you sure it's not a giant?'

'Well, I suppose it might…' started Laura but was cut off mid-sentence by Gemma chucking a pillow across the room into her face.

Outside rain was starting to fall, a gentle pitter-patter at first and then the sound of torrential cascades of water. A gutter dripped noisily just above the bedroom window. The two girls lay in bed without speaking, listening to the storm, both busy with their own thoughts.

If only Jamie's illness was as explainable as thunder, thought Laura, listening to the receding rumbles as the storm began to move away. It's every bit as devastating, but what is the point of it all? And if God is there why doesn't he do something? All those years in Sunday school and youth group and they tell you, don't worry about anything, just pray and God will help you. So why isn't he helping now? Doesn't he care?

She thought of all the times she and Jamie had argued. Even the last time they had been together, before he had begun to feel so ill on Wednesday night – was it really only Wednesday? – she had shouted at him because he had insisted on watching a programme on telly about the Olympics when she had wanted to watch Ant and Dec being interviewed on Midweek Chat. Supposing that was the last conversation they ever had? But then, she remembered, they had sat and drunk cold lemonade on the floor together and talked about school quite amicably. That's the thing about brothers, you hate them one minute and love them the next. It doesn't really matter which you're doing most of the time, because deep down you both know you care about each other. I guess that's why you need families, she thought, even if your dad's a sad relic of the Sixties, or worse still your mum's a house-proud neurotic, they're the only people who'll love you whatever you're like. Well, them and God, anyway.

It was nearly five o'clock in the morning and already light when she finally fell into a deep sleep. So deep was the sleep that when Gemma's mum tried to wake her a couple of hours later, she had to shake her shoulder and say her name several times to rouse her.

She sat up, yawning, and rubbing her eyes. For a moment she had no idea where she was, then it all came rushing back.

'Laura, pet,' Joanne was saying urgently, 'are you awake?' Laura had always thought how young and pretty Joanne was considering she was a mum, but this morning in her dressing-gown and without make-up she looked old and careworn. She sat down carefully on the bed, waiting for Laura to surface. 'Laura, your mum has just rung.' Her face was blotchy and there were suspicious streaks round her eyes.

All at once Laura knew what was coming.

'I'm afraid it's bad news. There's no way to say this gently, I just wish it wasn't me who had to tell you.' Joanne took a breath and made a noise in her throat which sounded as though she was trying to swallow a big lump. 'Jamie died at twenty to six this morning.'

She hugged Laura and began to cry quietly. Gemma, who had sat up under her duvet when her mum came in, climbed over piles of discarded clothes to Laura's bed and put her arms round both of them, weeping noisily.

So this is it, thought Laura, sitting as still as a statue and leaning against the pillow. It's happened, the thing I never really thought could happen.

Nothing is safe any more.

The rain had stopped, but outside the bedroom window the gutter was still dripping. Someone should get that fixed, she thought.

She gazed through a mist of tears over their heads out of the window at the pale sun which had risen as usual and where another Monday morning was beginning.

8

The next few days passed in a blur. Looking back on it later, Laura found that it was little details that she remembered best, rather than the big things.

Like the moment when she had arrived back at her own home with her dad later on the Monday afternoon and seeing Jamie's school blazer sitting on the hall chair where he always left it she had thought for a split second he must be upstairs changing out of his uniform the way he always did after school. There was the moment when she went to wash her face and suddenly caught sight of the bottle of aftershave she'd given him for Christmas, sitting on the bathroom shelf, virtually unused. It had smelt unspeakably vile, but he had never thrown it away for fear of hurting her feelings. There was the moment when she woke on Tuesday morning to the muffled sound of his radio alarm through the wall, permanently tuned to Radio One, the muted voice of the DJ on the breakfast show babbling away to an empty bedroom. And then there were all the moments when her mother sat at the kitchen table staring vacantly into space, as if she were trying to remember why she was there.

Laura herself cried very little. When she did it was more out of empathy for the desperate grief her parents were suffering than for herself. At times she found herself observing her own reactions and, disturbed at her own apparent lack of feeling, saying over and over to herself, Jamie is dead, my brother is dead. He's not coming back, ever. But somehow the words seemed meaningless. At night-time she lay awake for hours, thoughts going round and round her head, silly trivial thoughts, often nothing to do with Jamie.

The phone rang incessantly for the first two days and then it fell relatively silent. Hardly any of the calls were for Laura, and she began to wonder if anyone had told any of her friends about Jamie's death. Then cards and letters began to pour in, both for her and her parents, and she realised that she hadn't been forgotten, it was simply that no one could find the right words to say over the phone. I guess I'd feel the same if I was them, she thought.

There seemed to be no end to the things that had to be done after a death. Simon Redford, the vicar, came round two or three times, first to offer sympathy and support, and then to help plan the funeral. This proved to be more difficult than anticipated.

'Would you like to ask someone to read from the Bible?' he had asked Clare gently. 'A friend, or an uncle or something?'

But her mother had broken down at the suggestion. She just couldn't seem to get herself together sufficiently to make the decisions that had to be made. Surprisingly – considering how close he had been to Jamie – it was Clive who had been the calmer of the two. He had made a cup of tea for Clare, then taken the vicar to one side.

'I was wondering,' he said tentatively, 'it's all been such a shock – I mean we weren't expecting it like this – there's so much to think about. Couldn't we have the funeral service a bit later?'

Simon thought for a moment. 'Well you couldn't have a funeral service later,' he said, 'but you could always have a memorial service. People do that sometimes when someone young dies suddenly. It might actually be a really good thing in this case. I don't think Clare's ready to see lots of people, but a memorial service would provide a lovely opportunity for Jamie's own friends to come and celebrate his life. We could do it in September when everyone's back from their holidays. It would give you time to think really carefully about what you wanted to put in the service.'

'Yes, I think we'd like that, wouldn't we, Clare?' said Clive gratefully. 'Give us time to get used to the whole thing. What do you think? And Laura?'

Clare nodded, rotating her mug of tea in her hands. She looked as if she couldn't really care less. Laura said, 'Could some of the youth group take part? Noah and Clicker and everyone?'

'Of course,' said Simon. 'Whatever you like. In the meantime we'll make the funeral as simple and as brief as possible.'

He said a prayer with them and then left. Laura once again found herself wondering if God was listening.

'I thought you said Jamie Bevan wasn't going to die, miss,' said Rachel Ericson accusingly at registration on Wednesday morning.

Mrs Green looked harassed. 'I know, Rachel, I did say that, but I wasn't to know he was going to get an infection, the way he did, was I? It's such a rare thing to happen.'

'But you said the chemo would kill the cancer cells,' persisted Rachel, screwing up her forehead in an unaccustomed effort to remember the scientific facts which had been put before her. 'You said that once the cells were killed Jamie would recover.'

'Well, I was wrong,' said Mrs Green helplessly. 'The treatment made him extra open to infection and he just couldn't fight it off. Believe me, Rachel, I'm just as upset as you are, but I'm not God. I can't foresee everything that's going to happen. After all, any of us could die tomorrow, run over by a bus.'

'Yes, but he would've had time to think ahead wouldn't he, like, miss?' said Rachel. 'I mean if he'd *known* what was going to happen. He would've had time to get organised and work things out.'

'What kind of things?'

'Oh, I dunno,' said Rachel vaguely. She couldn't quite put it into words, but she felt sure that if she had been about to die there were things she would want to sort out. Things she would want to understand...

The day of the funeral had an extraordinarily surreal quality. Laura stood in the front pew of the church with her parents, the church where she had been every Sunday since she was very small, and tried not to look at the brown wooden coffin covered with flowers standing in the middle of the aisle. It was just too strange to imagine Jamie inside there. It was deeply weird to be in a place which was so familiar and yet to experience such unfamiliar feelings. Her mum and dad both cried a lot during the service and held each other's hands, but when they put their arms out to include her she felt awkward and alone, afraid of being washed away by the tide of their grief.

They sang a hymn and then the vicar talked about heaven and how they could all be grateful that Jamie's suffering was over, and what a wonderful talented caring person he'd been, his family must have been so proud of him. You obviously never saw him in one of his sulks when he didn't get his way, thought Laura, and immediately squashed the thought. You weren't supposed to remember bad things about the dead. She tried to imagine Jamie in heaven. Would he be the golden boy there, too, amongst all those angels? But then there'd be people like Mother Teresa and St Paul for him to compete with, by comparison he'd probably just seem quite ordinary.

They said some prayers and sang another hymn and the service was over.

The next bit was the hardest. She and her father and mother had to get back into the black funeral car which had brought them and drive to the cemetery for the burial. The hearse carrying Jamie's coffin went in front of them. The cemetery was on the other side of town so they had to drive very slowly through the streets of Stanworth to get there; the route took them almost straight past Laura's school. It was late afternoon, the time when most of her friends went home. They passed a gaggle of Year 12 students standing at the bus stop, most of them so busy talking that they barely noticed the funeral procession going by, but one boy looked up and caught Laura's eye as she went past. For a second he looked completely stunned, then tugged at the arms of his friends to point the car out to them, but already it had rounded a corner and Laura lost sight of them.

At the cemetery Jamie's coffin was lowered into the big freshly-dug grave and Simon said a few more prayers. Then the moment came for Laura and her parents to say goodbye. Together they came to the edge of the grave and peered in. Laura threw in a flower which the undertaker had given her.

What would happen to his body? she wondered. Presumably the coffin would rot away in a while, and Jamie with it. How long did it take for bones to disintegrate? Or perhaps they never did, didn't archaeologists sometimes find skeletons of people dating back hundreds of years? Shocked at her own thoughts, she stole a glance at her mother beside her. She was quite still, but occasionally a great racking sob would escape her. Clive stood with his arm round her, weeping quietly, an unaccustomed sight in a dark suit and tie.

Back at home they sat in the living-room with her grand-mother and Jamie's godfather, drinking tea and trying to eat cake. After a while Laura could stand the silence no longer and went to see if there were any messages left on the phone. There was one from Gemma, she must have rung while they were at the funeral.

'Hallo, Laura, it's me, Gemma. I've just got back from school. I thought you might be feeling a bit down, so here I am. Give us a ring if you want a chat.' There was a pause, and the sound of murmuring voices in the background. Gemma's voice came back on the line. 'We're all here, thinking of you, me and Michelle and Noah and Clicker and Alan and everyone. Look, I know you're feeling really pants, but we all just want to say we love you, right? OK.' Then a click.

It was good to hear them. Laura started to dial Gemma's number, but halfway through was overwhelmed with a huge feeling of tiredness. She would ring later. She didn't really feel up to Gemma's extravagant expressions of sympathy just at the moment. An enormous gulf seemed to have grown between her and her friends. How could she ever feel close to anyone again who hadn't experienced what she was experiencing?

A few days after the funeral Laura sat on Jamie's bed, looking at the big cherry tree outside his window. She had always hankered after this room ever since she could remember, it was so much larger than hers and had a much nicer view; hers looked out sideways onto the garage. The thought crossed her mind that she could sleep in this room now if she wanted. She had never wanted anything less in her life.

Clare was kneeling on the floor, going through Jamie's chest of drawers, from time to time giving a surreptitious sniff. When she spoke it was with an unnatural cheerfulness.

'Oh look, Laura, here's the old jumper Jamie used to wear in bed when it was cold. I wondered what had happened to that. And his Snoopy socks.' She glanced up at her daughter who was sitting in a hunched position cradling her knees. 'Is there anything you want? To remind you of him?'

Laura shook her head.

'Only, now's your opportunity if you want to have a couple of his things. Anything you like, clothes, or a picture from the wall or something?'

Laura said nothing.

Her mother sighed. 'Look, sweetheart, I know this isn't much fun, but we're going to have to clear his stuff out sometime, and the longer we leave it the harder it's going to get.' She stuffed several pairs of socks into a bin bag.

Quite unexpectedly Laura found herself feeling ridiculously angry. 'How can you be so callous!' she burst out. 'He's only been gone less than two weeks and already you're clearing him all away! As if he was just a pile of dirty washing! Do you think that by emptying his drawers you can just make him disappear out of our lives?'

'Of course not,' said her mum, her face clouding over with distress, 'you know I don't think that. Laura, you've been so quiet all the time, Dad and I just don't know what you're feeling. We haven't even seen you cry apart from a few tears at the funeral. You haven't got to keep it all in, you know.'

But that was just it. She had got to keep it all in. She was too scared to think, *really* think, in case it all got too much to cope with. It was as if she was watching a film in which she was supposed to have a starring role, but if she let the role take her over and began to experience all the emotions that went with it, it would all become too painful. It was safer to just act the part without feeling it, pretending it was nothing to do with her.

And then there was this niggling demon that lurked at the back of her brain and whispered *They loved Jamie best, you know. It should have been you, not Jamie.*

But she mustn't listen to that demon, not ever.

Her mother came and sat on the bed beside her and put an arm round her, hugging her tightly. 'We've all got to help each other, sweetheart. Where would I be if I didn't have you?'

Laura put out her hand onto the bed to steady herself, and her fingers closed over Jamie's cap which he always kept tucked under the pillow, the cap he wore after he started to lose his hair. She pulled it out and buried her face in it. It smelt of the sun-block he had smeared on his head in his last week when the sun had got so strong. It was a strong coconutty smell, and it reminded her of how she had sat with him in the garden one afternoon, eating cake and watching a procession of ants marching across the patio carrying some of the dropped crumbs to their nest.

'As if each knew exactly what their particular job in life was,' she'd said, watching them with fascination. 'Even if we were to tread on them in the next minute they'd have done their work.'

'Of course. It is their destiny,' Jamie had replied in his best Star Wars voice.

'Ants don't have destinies, blockhead.'

'These ones do. Look at them, it's obvious. They're all working together to help each other.'

Laura had leaned over from her garden chair to watch them more carefully. There were hundreds of them, some apparently working together and others working round each other.

'Like us in the Halfway House,' she'd said.

'Yeah, just like that. Which is why you mustn't stand on any of them. They all need each other.'

'So what'll they do if I squash one?' she'd said nastily.

'Oh, they'll close ranks eventually,' he'd said airily. 'Of course their pecking order won't be the same any more, and some of them may have to learn new skills to compensate, but they'll still work as a team. Life will go on.'

'And where did you learn all about the habits of ants, Mr Cleverpants?'

'Observation. They're just like people really.'

Only three weeks ago.

Sitting on his bed now, holding his cap and remembering the feeling of the sun and the taste of the cake, Laura felt her throat go dry and tight.

Life will go on.

Without warning, a torrent of tears gushed up and she began to cry as if she would never stop.

9

Noah had a theory that when you were really angry the best thing to do was go for a run. There was something about pounding along a footpath, hot and sweaty from exertion, which helped you to let off steam and rant and rave to yourself till you were exhausted. It also gave you a good space for thinking; your thoughts could scurry through your head unchecked in time with the beat of your footsteps on the pavement.

Noah was very angry today. It was over two weeks since Jamie had died and he'd been feeling angry nearly all the time since his dad had broken the news to him over breakfast on that dreadful Monday.

There were two reasons for his anger. Firstly he was mad at God for taking away his best friend for no apparent reason. He felt an all-consuming rage at the thought that Jamie would never achieve all the things he'd planned, that all the experiences he'd had and all the things he'd learnt were completely wasted. And secondly Noah was angry with himself for not being able to handle his feelings better. He had always been looked up to by the rest of the gang as being the one who had his faith sorted out, the one who knew the right thing to say in a crisis and who would smooth things over with a joke when people fell out. So where were the answers now, the Christian responses to the questions that no one was saying out loud but everyone was secretly asking? He'd tried talking first to his mum and then his dad, both of them usually knew what to say when things went wrong, but this time they were as much at a loss as he was. And that was another thing that made him angry – he thought Christian parents like his should be ready with some neat solution – maybe a Bible verse, or at least a holy thought – to put things right when it was needed, but they had utterly failed.

So Noah ran. Every day he came home from school and put on his running shorts and his trainers and did the circuit round one side of the town. He always did the same route: to the end of his road, past the church and the primary school, along the canal for a bit, then up towards the shopping parade and back along the path which ran round the far side of the park. It took him about thirty-five minutes from start to finish.

Today's run was different because the council were re-laying the footpath in the park. This meant that he had to take a detour round the crazy golf pitch and the public conveniences to get to the entrance, making his route a bit longer than usual. He was running so fast down the shortcut behind the toilets he almost ran full tilt into a very startled Lee, who was just in the process of painting a cartoon figure on the brick wall with a can of black spray paint. Caught in the act.

'Ha!' shouted Noah. 'So it *was* you who sprayed pictures all over the club building! I'd recognise your style anywhere!'

'Prove it then,' said Lee. He stood back for a moment to admire his handiwork, then started to paint a second figure next to the first.

'Yeah, prove it,' echoed Vinny, suddenly materialising from the side of the building. He was clearly supposed to be acting as watch-out but had temporarily left his post to give his full attention to a bag of mini dough-nuts. Noah shrugged his shoulders. He knew it was pointless to get into an argument with them, and although he was probably miles fitter than they were he didn't fancy his chances in a two-against-one fight. He prepared to run on, but Lee stopped him.

'Hey, hang about. Wasn't it one of your mates died last week? Weird looking bloke with the strange hair-cut? In the paper and that?'

'Yes. He was my best friend,' said Noah shortly.

'Woss that all about, then? What did he die from?'

'He had leukaemia.'

'Oh,' said Lee rubbing his nose where a splash of paint had landed. He looked quite comical with black smeared all over his face, not at all threatening, in fact. The sight was absurd enough to encourage Noah to ask him some more questions.

'Do you know anything about the fire? I know you were somewhere else when it happened, but do you know who did it?'

A guarded look came over Lee's face. 'I might do.'

'Bit of a barbecue, eh?' sniggered Vinny, but Lee said, 'Pack it in, Vinny.' Then to Noah, 'Do the police know who it was?'

'They've got their suspicions. Strong suspicions,' said Noah. 'If you know something, you should tell them.'

'Yeah, but then I'd be in trouble, wouldn't I, mate,' said Lee. 'So you see I can't say anything.' He stopped spraying, his cartoon finished, and put the can on the grass. 'But look, I'm sorry about your pal. Was there a funeral or something?'

'There was, but it was only for the family.' Noah had not been invited to the funeral, only Laura and her parents and grandparents had gone to it, but his dad had told him there would be a big Thanksgiving Service in September when everyone was back from their summer holidays. He was secretly quite relieved not to have been to the funeral, he didn't think he could have coped with it. Adults crying and everyone talking in hushed voices and all that sort of stuff.

And Jamie inside a box.

He began to feel angry again, time to run on. But something about the second cartoon figure made him pause a little longer, a certain familiarity.

'It's me!' he exclaimed. No doubt about it, running shorts, long legs, exaggeratedly big grin, black wavy hair. It's always harder to recognise yourself than someone else in a drawing, but this was unmistakable in spite of the bumpy background.

'Might be,' said Lee.

'He can do *anyone*,' put in Vinny. 'Anyone at all. Jus' name them, an' he does 'em.'

'Unbelievable,' said Noah, really impressed. 'You could make something of that. Hasn't someone at school told you how good you are?' He started to jog on the spot, ready to take off again.

'He doesn't do school,' explained Vinny.

'What d'you mean, doesn't do school?'

'Like I said. Never goes. Me neither. Haven't been for months.'

'What, you mean you've left?'

'Not exactly. We jus' don't *do* it.'

What a pair of losers, muttered Noah to himself under his breath as he ran on down the path. But an idea was beginning to form in his head.

The term had come to an end and the summer holidays stretched out endlessly ahead. For the young people of St Michael's, life had gone on hold. There was no club to go to, and they couldn't even start decorating again until the structure of the building had been thoroughly checked and the insurance company had finished assessing the fire damage. In the meantime they were reduced to visiting each other's houses or hanging about in the park with a football. Some of them disappeared away on holiday with their families, so that the ones who were left had to make do with whoever was around, even if they weren't particularly close friends.

A week into the holidays, Clicker was sitting in front of the computer working on the Halfway House website when he had a phone-call from Laura.

'Do you want to come round here this evening? I'm going mad sitting here with nothing to do. Gemma's coming over and Alan and maybe a couple of the others. Not Noah – he's gone camping in Devon.'

'Yeah, sure. That is, if you really want us,' said Clicker, cautiously.

'Course I do,' said Laura. She was getting a lot of this kind of reaction from friends at the moment. As if having a normal evening with a few mates might somehow make her into some kind of unfeeling monster. They didn't seem to understand that normality was what she needed more than anything else.

She was waiting at the front gate when Clicker arrived.

'Come on in,' she said, lifting the latch. 'I've got a surprise for you.'

He went through into the back room to find Gemma, Alan and Sophie Illingworth already there. And...

'Robbie!'

Robbie it was. 'I was just, you know, passing,' he explained, fidgeting with a cushion on his lap. 'Laura was there in the road talking to Alan and she kind of asked me in. If you don't mind,' he added nervously.

Clicker blinked at him in some amazement. 'Mind? Why should I mind?'

'Well, not you specially, but everyone. 'Cause of Lee and everything. And the fire.'

'He thinks we're blaming him,' said Gemma. 'I've been telling him we know it wasn't him. He wasn't anywhere near when it happened, was he?'

'It was Max and Dennis wasn't it?' said Laura. 'They've completely vanished since then, so it must've been them.'

Robbie looked very uncomfortable. 'I can't be sure. I just know they were planning something – some of the stuff they said made me realise they were going to do something really bad.'

'So it was you who rang and gave the warning,' said Gemma, 'and if it hadn't been for that the whole building would've burned down. That was really brave.'

'What warning?' asked Robbie in surprise.

'You know, the warning that someone was going to do something to the club. Someone rang the police. It must've been you. Unless someone else knew.'

'I never phoned anyone,' said Robbie, 'I wanted to, but I was afraid of what they might do to me. It wasn't me.'

'Then who was it?'

'Haven't a clue. No one else knew. Except Lee and Vinny, of course.'

There was a moment's pause, then Laura said slowly, 'Could it have been *Lee*?'

'He's not all bad, you know,' said Robbie. 'I mean he seems so hard and like he hates the whole world, but there's another side to him that not many people see. He has a really rough time at home – he lives up on the Greenfield estate and his mum has this bloke who drinks all the time. Although Lee won't say anything about it I'm sure she gets thumped sometimes. I've seen her in Quickmart with a big black eye and her collar all up so you couldn't see the rest of her face.'

'So how did Lee get in with Max?'

'Max doesn't live round here. He sells stuff – you know, off the back of a lorry kind of stuff. He and Dennis visit the area for a few days till they get rid of it all and then move on. They come and go quite a lot, they've visited here two or three times in the last couple of months. Anyway Max found Lee and the other guys hanging around on a street corner back in April and reckoned they might know the right sort of people he could persuade to buy a job lot of electrical equipment.'

'But Lee's only sixteen. He doesn't have those kind of contacts.'

'You'd be surprised. There's some pretty dodgy people living on the Greenfield.'

'And what about Vinny?' asked Sophie.

Robbie grinned. 'Oh, Vinny. Vinny's not really evil – although he'd love you to think he is. He just seems to have to do everything Lee tells him. If you could get him away from Lee he might even develop a mind of his own.'

'And what about you?' asked Laura. 'Do you do everything Lee tells you?'

Robbie pulled at the cushion so hard that a tassel came off in his hand. 'Maybe not. But you gotta understand, things are exciting with Lee. Not like going to church and being good and doing everything right like when I hung out with you lot in the old days. You never know what's going to happen with Lee, he gets these really crazy ideas and we're always having a laugh. You should get to know him.' He stood up. 'I can't stay. But I might look in when you start decorating the club again, could I do that? I'd like to see it properly.'

'No problem,' said Alan, 'any time. We don't know how soon we'll be able to get back in, but you'll be able to tell when we're there by the noise. And p'raps you could persuade Lee and friends to leave us alone this time.'

'I doubt it. But I'll see what I can do.' Robbie gave an embarrassed smile. 'Catch you later. And thanks for not beating my head in.'

Noah had forgotten what a long way it was to Devon. Every year he and his family trekked down to the same camp-site where they hired a mobile home and a tent for a fortnight. The campsite overlooked a sandy cove and had marvellous views of the sun setting, at least it did when the sun bothered to shine. All too often it poured with rain and the family spent their evenings huddled in the caravan playing board games while the younger children sat on their bunks and argued over their Lego. It was always a terrible squash. In the earlier years they had all managed in a tent, but as the family grew larger Sue had insisted they needed running water and a toilet so they had graduated to a caravan. Now that there were six children, the parents slept in a tiny tent while the children all crammed into the mobile home.

They always drove to Devon in Ben's van, an ancient vehicle which only just managed to pass its MOT each year. It had started out in life as a small mini-bus, but Ben had adapted it to take his family, removing some of the seats to make more luggage space. This year Noah's exceptionally long legs had earned him a place in the front passenger seat next to his dad, while the rest of the family sat in the back with Sue in the middle to break up fights.

'You OK?' said Ben looking sideways at his eldest son after they had travelled some way. Noah had been unusually quiet.

'Yeah, I'm fine. I was just thinking about things.'

'It's been a tough month.'

'You're not kidding. First the fire and then Jamie.'

'How're you feeling now?'

Noah considered. 'A bit better. Though I still can't understand why it happened. About Jamie, I mean.'

Ben sighed. 'Me neither. They've asked me to help put together the memorial service, you know. I've been racking my brains to think of how to do it. Perhaps you might come up with some ideas?'

'Me? How would I know anything? I've never had a friend die before.'

'That's why you might be able to help me. We all feel the same; death is something we never normally think about. The old cliché about it always happening to someone else, not someone you really care about.'

'Yeah. Well, I'll think. But don't expect any brainwaves.' Noah was silent for a moment then added, 'It's strange, you know, we all reacted in different ways. Gemma was all emotional and Laura went all quiet. I got angry and Clicker just seemed to want to pretend nothing had happened. Michelle was like that too when we first knew Jamie was ill. She actually ignored him in school.'

Ben nodded. 'Some people do react like that. They are just so shocked by what's happening they're embarrassed by their own emotions. They find it easier to behave as though life is still normal. I bet Michelle's kicking herself now that she wasn't brave enough to talk about it.'

'I guess she is. She's making a huge effort to be nice to Laura.'

There was a shriek from the back seat. The twins were fighting over a toy and one of them had resorted to using his teeth in an effort to wrest it away from his sister.

'Davey, don't do that,' said Sue wearily. 'Give it back to Mel. Now.'

'Are we nearly there?' asked a plaintive voice.

'Time for emergency supplies, I think,' said Ben hastily reaching out to the shelf next to the steering wheel and passing back a bag of apples and a bottle of squash. Sue distributed rations round the van.

'I was thinking,' said Noah as an uneasy peace returned. 'About the club. Are we going to just do it like it was before? 'Cause there's going to be a big gap where Jamie's photos would have gone.'

His father glanced at him quickly, then looked away. 'Why? Have you another idea?'

'Well… yes, I have as a matter of fact. It's Lee.' Ben gave a startled look but Noah went on. 'Did you know he was a fantastic artist?'

'I remember the cartoons on the club door when we started painting. I presume that was Lee.'

'It was. He's actually really brilliant. I've seen some others that he's done, and they're really clever. He seems to have the knack of catching someone's personality in just a few lines. I was wondering…'

'What?'

'Well, couldn't we get him to do what Jamie was going to do, but instead of photos it could be actual drawings, straight onto the wall? Like a mural?'

'It's possible,' said his father thoughtfully. He seemed to be considering whether to say something more. He glanced into his driving mirror to see whether any of the other children were listening but they were all preoccupied with I Spy and squabbles about who had the biggest apple. Lowering his voice so that no one but Noah could hear he said, 'As a matter of fact I've had a bit of news about the club. Quite exciting news.'

'What news?'

'You remember Miranda Jukes was supposed to open the club that Saturday.'

'Yes, of course, I do.'

'Well, by the time I was able to contact her to stop her coming she was already all psyched up for the occasion so she came anyway.'

'What do you mean? How can she have? There was nothing to open.'

'I know. So instead I took her up to the club to show her the damage and what it would have been like. She was nearly as upset as we were when she saw what had happened.'

'And? The exciting news?'

'Yesterday, when we were packing for this holiday I had a phone-call from her secretary. She's decided to bring her makeover team to completely redo the whole thing. With all the resources she has at her command she can do it in less than a week, all the electrics and the re-plastering and everything.'

Noah's eyes widened. 'Wow!'

'Wow just about describes it. But you mustn't tell anyone, it's all going to be a surprise.' He glanced in his mirror again.

Noah spent a few moments mulling over this spectacular piece of information. Then he said, 'But if Lee did some artwork we'd have to tell him all about it, and I shouldn't think he'd be able to keep his trap shut for longer than thirty seconds. Can you see him missing a chance to brag to Vinny and Robbie and co?'

Ben grinned. 'It would be tempting for him,' he admitted, 'but I think he might surprise us. It could be a risk worth taking.' Ignoring Noah's sceptical expression he added, 'The question is, how will he manage to produce drawings of everyone if he doesn't get them to model for him?'

Noah thought about this. 'It may be possible,' he said at last, 'I think we have loads of snaps from youth group outings in the past that he might be able to work from. And some of us he actually knows by sight, like me and Clicker and Gemma. I'm sure there are others.'

'Well, it's worth a try,' said Ben. 'It could be a perfect way to get to bridge the gap between him and us. We'll work on it when we get home.'

'*Dad*,' came an urgent voice from the back, 'I need a wee-wee. I need one *now*!'

Ben scanned the horizon for a service station. There was one coming up in just under a mile. 'We'll stop in a minute,' he called back. He indicated to move into the slow lane and said to Noah, 'Now don't forget, not a word to anyone.'

Noah tapped the side of his nose. 'I know nuzzing,' he said in a passable imitation of Manuel from *Fawlty Towers*. 'Your secret's safe with me.'

10

By the time Noah got home from Devon the GCSE results were out. They were boringly predictable, Clicker had done really well, and Noah had some reasonable grades. It was strange for them to think that Jamie should have been collecting his too.

A week before the memorial service, Laura's dad had a phone call from Ben. Laura and her mum, watching television in the next room, listened to Clive's end of the conversation.

'No,' he said, after listening for a few moments. 'We hadn't really thought... I don't know... if you think it would work. Would you put it together? ... no, I doubt it ... too soon ... well, I could ask her, I suppose.'

There was another pause, then he said, 'OK I'll run it past them both. Thanks a lot, Ben, I'll be in touch.'

'What was that about?' asked Laura as he came through into the living room.

'The memorial service.' He sat down on the sofa. 'Ben thought it might make it rather special if some of Jamie's friends came up to the front and said a few words about him. So that it's not all just adults holding forth. What do you think?'

'Great idea,' said Laura immediately. 'What do you think, Mum?'

'It's a thought,' said Clare. She was beginning to take a

little more interest in what was happening around her, but still seemed to find it hard to make any decisions. 'Who does he have in mind?'

'Well, Noah, of course, and maybe Gemma, she's never short of things to say. And if they both spoke then probably Clicker ought to have a word.'

'Clicker would never do that,' said Laura decisively. Clicker hadn't even acknowledged straight out to her that Jamie was dead. Whenever they met he talked about absolutely anything that came into his head except the thing that they both knew was most important to them. It was as if Jamie had just never existed. At first Laura was seriously hurt by this, but in time she began to realise that it didn't mean Clicker didn't care, it was just that he couldn't find the right words. At any rate, the thought of him standing up in a church service and talking about his friend was inconceivable.

'What about you, Laura?' asked her dad. 'Could you say something?'

Laura shook her head. 'I don't think so – what would I say? About what a great guy he was and that sort of stuff?'

'Not necessarily. Just the truth,' said Clive. 'Or maybe something about how God has helped you through a bad time?'

Laura said nothing. She wasn't sure yet that God *had* helped her through a bad time. The only people who had really helped her were her friends, just by being around and doing things with her when it all got too much. Even Clicker was kind of comforting in his own way; his awkward silence seemed to transmit a sort of reassurance that he knew how difficult things were for her. As if he realised that Jamie's death was too devastating to be talked about the way you talked about what was for dinner or who was going to be chucked out next from the *Big Brother* house.

'I don't know,' she said, 'I'll have to think about it.'

'No need to decide now,' said her dad, 'you can make up your mind nearer the time. But what you could help me do is choose some of the music. Which were the songs he liked best? Are they the sort of thing we could play at the service?'

'There's still some of his CDs in his room,' said Clare, 'I left them there when I was clearing up. There might be something there that would be suitable. Perhaps Laura could look through them.' She spoke with some effort.

'Would it have to be Christian music?' asked Laura.

'I don't think so. We want to celebrate his whole life, not just his church life,' said Clive.

Laura nodded approvingly. It would seem kind of strange to do just religious stuff as if that was all there had been to Jamie. In fact, really, when you thought about it you couldn't actually separate the Christian going-to-church Jamie from the everyday going-to-school and mad-on-photography-and-sport Jamie. They were all muddled up together.

'I'll have a look and see what's there,' she said.

The service took place on the last Friday of the summer holidays. St Michael's was the main parish church for Stanworth and was quite large, but on that Friday there wasn't an empty seat in the place. By the time the service began people were squashed into every corner of the building, some having to stand at the back. Many of the regular congregation were there, people of all ages, friends of Clive and Clare and friends of Laura. Most of the youth group turned up and a surprisingly large contingent from Jamie's school, including his form teacher, Mrs Green, and the headmaster.

Gemma, sitting near the front and waiting for the service to begin, craned her neck to try and get a better view of all the faces behind her.

'Don't stare,' hissed Clicker, sitting next to her.

'But I have to see who's here,' she whispered back, frustrated to find her vision of the opposite side of the church obscured by a row of pillars. Just as she was about to give up and concentrate on looking at the service sheet she caught sight of three familiar figures standing in the furthest corner at the back of the building.

'Clicker!' she whispered fiercely. 'Look! Look who's there!'

'Can't see anything,' he replied, hardly bothering to turn round.

'Look! Over there, dumbo. Lee and Vinny! By the stone thingy at the back. Can't you see them? And Robbie. They're all there. Why do you think they've come? They hardly even knew Jamie.'

'Robbie did,' said Clicker. 'Don't you remember they were at primary school together? P'raps the others just tagged along with him.'

Gemma was prevented from saying any more by the sound of the organ starting to play.

It was a tune which they both vaguely recognised but neither could put a name to: rich powerful music, kind of sad and happy all at the same time. Laura and her parents arrived while it was playing and took their places in the front pew and Gemma found herself feeling sorry for Laura at having to be in the hot seat yet again.

As the last notes of the organ died away, Ben came to stand at the front.

'A very warm welcome to you all,' he said, 'and especially to Jamie's family.' He smiled at Clive, Clare and Laura. 'This is a very important occasion, a day when we meet together to remember a young man who has played a very big part in the life of this town and particularly of this church; and I hope that later in the service we're going to hear from some of his friends just what he meant to them. But first of all we're going to pray.'

Prayers followed and some songs and a poem from a boy in Jamie's class. Then the headmaster got up to read from the Bible. As he started to read, a deep silence fell upon his listeners.

'...if I have a faith that can move mountains, but have not love, I am nothing. If I give all I possess to the poor and have not love, I gain nothing.

'Love is patient, love is kind. It does not envy, it does not boast, it is not proud... Love does not delight in evil but rejoices with truth. It always protects, always trusts, always hopes, always perseveres.'

Laura, wedged between her parents and staring at her folded hands on her lap, looked up at these words.

'...Love never fails... When I was a child, I talked like a child, I thought like a child, I reasoned like a child. When I became a man, I put childish ways behind me. Now we see but a poor reflection as in a mirror; but then we shall see face to face. Now I know in part; then I shall know fully, even as I am fully known.'

The headmaster finished reading and passed the microphone to the vicar. Simon looked round at his congregation.

'I expect some of you remember watching Princess Diana's funeral on television. This passage from the Bible was read then, too. It's a very appropriate reading to have when someone dies unexpectedly, because the question we all ask is "Why?" Why did this happen to someone so young, to someone who had so much to give? And the only answer I can give to you is that there *is* no answer. Even St Paul knew that. We're like children, he says, we only know things in part, we don't have the whole picture, we think like children and try to work things out like children.

'If death was the end of the road we might as well all give up now. But it isn't. It's only a stopping place, a kind of halfway house if you like—' he paused for a second and gave a fleeting smile to the three rows of youth group at the front '—a door that has to be gone through between this life and the next. And in the next life we *will* understand, because we'll see God face to face. Just as Jamie can now know fully, even as he is fully known, to use the words of the passage.'

Gemma stole a glance down the pew at Noah. He was gazing at the vicar in deep concentration.

'So what is there to help those of us who are left behind to make sense of life while we're here on earth?' Simon went on. 'Well, I think it has to be this thing called love. God's love for us and ours for each other. We may not understand why God allows these tragic things to happen, but we can always be sure he loves us. We can be sure he does because we experience it every day in the way he guides us and looks after us, and in the way that our friends care for us, and of course because he sent Jesus to suffer just as we do and to die for us. And if we can show that same love to others, even if we don't think they deserve it, we will begin to get nearer to understanding how God works. Love that isn't envious or boastful or self-seeking, but love which looks for the best in everyone and continues to hope where there is no hope. It's through the love of others that we find what God's love is like, and it's through loving others that we can pass that on to the rest of the world.'

Gemma nudged Clicker. 'Even Lee?' she muttered.

'Sssh,' he whispered back severely.

Simon continued for a few more minutes. 'We are all going to miss Jamie terribly,' he said finally. 'There will be days when we think we are getting over it, then something will happen or someone will say something to remind us of him and we will feel as if the grief is starting all over again. Those are the moments when we have to hang onto the fact that God loves us, that he is still with us, even if it doesn't feel like it, and he will bring us through.' He paused and smiled at Laura and her mum and dad. 'That's what faith is. Believing something to be true even when you can't be sure and living in the light of that belief. So, these three remain: faith, hope and love. But the greatest of these is love.'

He sat down.

It was Ben's turn to come to the front and speak again. 'Just a few of my own memories of Jamie; then I'll give some other people a turn. Jamie was a great guy, always in the centre of every gathering, a natural leader. He had loads of friends in the youth group and was never short of new ideas about ways to improve things. The thing that upsets me most—' he drew a breath and for a moment looked as though he might not be able to go on '—the thing that upsets me most is that he will never see the finished club. He had so many plans for it.'

He stopped abruptly and turned to his son. 'Noah.'

Noah went and stood beside him. 'Jamie was my best friend,' he said, 'I don't know that I can say much more than that. What Simon said about love and it being there in our friends and all that was true. Being mates with Jamie made me feel like I was someone special, he was always there for me and I hope he felt I was always there for him. When he died I just couldn't believe it, I got dead angry at God and shouted at him a lot.' He grinned and added, 'But God didn't seem to mind too much. Anyway he's got his work cut out now, keeping Jamie in order in heaven.' He glanced down nervously at Clare but she was smiling at him.

Gemma was next. 'Jamie was well fit,' she began. A ripple of laughter ran through the congregation. 'Well, he was,' she said defensively, 'all the girls thought so, didn't we girls? I really fancied him. But the thing is,' she went on, avoiding Laura's eye, 'in the end who you fancy and who you don't fancy doesn't seem very important when you're thinking about life and death and big things like that. You begin to realise that there's more important things than looking gorgeous and keeping up with the latest gear. So for me the thing I will remember most about Jamie was that he was my friend, just like he was to Noah.'

Ben retrieved the mike from her and turned to Laura. 'Do you want to say anything?'

Laura hesitated a moment, then climbed out of her pew over several pairs of legs and joined Ben on the steps.

'He could be really annoying,' she said without preamble, 'whenever there was a new packet of biscuits, he always pinched the chocolate ones from the tin before I could get to them. He was better at everything than me. Sometimes he laughed when I didn't understand things as quickly as him. He was always nicking my CDs. But he was kind too, he often helped me with my homework. And he understood when things weren't good at school. We had jokes which no one... He was just... oh, I don't know... he was just my brother.' Her eyes were bright with tears and she scowled in a huge effort of will to prevent them from falling.

Ben put a hand on her shoulder. 'Thanks, Laura,' he said quietly, 'that was great. Clicker?' But Clicker was shaking his head vigorously and trying to shrink down into his seat so that no one would see him.

One of Jamie's school-friends sang a song, then there were a couple of excerpts from his favourite CDs. After that there were a few more prayers, a final hymn and the service was over.

Afterwards a big tea was served in the hall. As the congregation filed through from the church, Ben caught sight of Lee, Vinny and Robbie trying to slip out of the back entrance without being noticed.

'Hey, guys!' he called, nimbly climbing over several seats to get past the slow moving crowd. 'Wait a sec! I want to talk to you.'

Gemma, watching from a distance, saw him disappear through the big main door of the church into the street with the three boys.

'Wonder what's going on there,' she said to Michelle who was pressed up against her in the queue for tea and sandwiches.

'Probably in trouble again,' said Michelle, leaning across the table to help herself from a plate of food, adding, 'Don't touch the ham ones, they've been in my mum's freezer since her birthday party in May.' She took a large mouthful of ginger cake. 'They're a right bunch of no-hopers, those three. Wouldn't be surprised if they're wanted by the law.'

Several minutes elapsed before Ben re-appeared. There was no sign of the three youths. He pushed his way through to a space at the side of the hall where he thumped on the floor with a broom handle and then climbed on a chair.

'Can I have everyone's attention a moment,' he said loudly. 'I have something very important to say.' The buzz of conversation died down. 'Probably this isn't the best moment to announce this,' said Ben, 'but I can't think of another time when we'll have the whole church family together. I just wanted to tell you all that we are ready to start work again on the club and it would be wonderful if we could begin again with a bang. I'm hoping that all the young people will turn up to help on the first evening, yes, *all* of you, and that the rest of you, mums, dads and everyone else will come along too just for a few minutes so that we can officially commit the work to God. Can I ask you to do that? It's really very crucial that all the young people should be there.'

There was an undercurrent of chatter. 'Which night are we talking, Ben?' asked someone.

'Oh sorry, forgot to say. Wednesday night, 7 o'clock, this coming week. Can you all do it?'

'Rather short notice isn't it, Ben?' said one of the older ladies, 'Wednesday's my keep fit night.'

'It's only for a few minutes,' said Ben, 'you won't have to stay long. You won't regret it. I'm sorry to use Jamie's special service to make an announcement like this, but the whole project was very close to his heart so I don't think he'd mind.'

'We'll be there!' called Joanne. She turned to her husband Steve and said, 'It's exciting, isn't it? A fresh start? At least we'll all be a bit more experienced in what we're doing this time.'

'I suppose you want me to stay home with Jodie while you're out gallivanting with your paintbrush again,' groaned Steve. 'Just when I thought you'd be at home a bit more.'

'Oh, don't be such a big baby,' said Joanne impatiently. 'You know what a great project it is. I know you're as excited as me deep down.'

'I am, am I? And I suppose I'm meant to be grateful to have a wife who understands me so well,' sighed Steve. 'All I can say is it's lucky I have such a taste for microwave dinners.'

11

'Good evening to you all and a very warm welcome to *Just Up Your Street*. Tonight we have a very special programme lined up for you, something rather out of the ordinary.'

Miranda Jukes turned sideways for a different camera shot. She was wearing a sleeveless stripey vest and a pair of cropped trousers, and her short blonde hair was stylishly tousled.

'Could do with a good hairbrush, if you ask me,' said Clare, perched on a stool about three feet away from the television.

'Mu-um. It's meant to look like that.' Laura glared at her from the floor.

It was Saturday evening nearly a month after the memorial service and over a dozen people were crammed into the Bevans' back room, watching television. The sound had been turned up and the video was busy recording. A new video – the old one had never truly recovered from its unsolicited Big Mac. A terminal case of indigestion was how Clive had put it.

The camera closed in on Miranda. She was standing in a studio surrounded by cardboard scaffolding and step ladders. A giantsize paint-pot, nearly twice her height, stood behind her, fake paint dripping down its side. She stepped over a huge paintbrush which had been artily draped across the floor and spoke confidentially to her unseen audience.

'Just six months ago the youth group at St Michael's church in Stanworth inherited a derelict pub to use as a drop-in centre and youth club. The group managed to raise enough money to do up the building and spent all their spare time working to create a wonderful place for the young people in the area to come to after school, a place where they could make new friends, learn new skills and generally keep off the streets. Unfortunately,' her voice dropped several tones, 'on the very day it was due to be opened – by me, actually, as it happens—' her face took on its most sincere expression '—there was a fire and much of the building was destroyed.'

'There it is!' shouted Alan as the picture changed to Devonshire Hill, zooming into a shot of the Halfway House with blackened windows, partly screened by boarding.

Miranda's voice continued in the background. 'The club was badly damaged. There was no way it could open in that state. Much of the kitchen and some of the back room had been destroyed.' Another shot, this time of the interior, Ben in jeans and Miranda in an immaculate white boiler suit picking their way around the burnt-out debris.

'When was that, Ben?' asked Sophie Illingworth. 'You never told us you'd taken her round there.'

'There's lots of things I don't tell you,' replied Ben enigmatically.

There were further shots of Miranda walking round the building, pointing out specific points of damage and talking about the kind of materials that had been used in doing it up, then the scene reverted to the studio.

'It was going to take the young people several more weeks to do the place up all over again and they'd already been working at it for months.' She turned to yet another camera and smiled conspiratorially. 'So that's where we decided to step in.'

More footage followed showing how she and her team had smuggled in their equipment and got to work.

'There's that van that sat outside the building for four days!' exclaimed Gemma. 'It was *their* van. And you told us it belonged to the electrician, Ben.'

'He's a good liar when he wants to be,' chuckled Noah.

'You're a fine one to talk,' said Clicker accusingly, 'you knew about it all the time, and never told anyone.'

'Shush,' said Michelle, 'this is the bit where we come in.'

Miranda stood on the pavement outside the Halfway House occasionally casting furtive glances to either side of her and speaking in a stage whisper.

'…And this is the moment we've been waiting for. Any minute now the young people are going to arrive, thinking they're about to start work, and they're going to find it's all been done for them! I'm just waiting here to see who comes…'

She broke off as a whistling Clicker wandered into view, hands in pockets. She beamed at him and waved a microphone under his nose. 'Hallo. Are you here to start work on the club?'

Clicker looked at the microphone in some puzzlement. 'What the—?'

'You know who I am, don't you?' asked Miranda, barely able to keep the excitement out of her voice.

'No,' said Clicker, bemused, 'should I?' This was greeted by a huge burst of laughter from the viewers.

'Good old Clicker. Bloomin' typical.'

'What planet are you off, Clicker?'

'It's not *my* fault,' said Clicker, aggrieved, 'just 'cause I don't watch these stupid programmes. I can't know who everyone is, can I?'

'Look, here comes Gemma!' interrupted Laura as Gemma appeared onscreen behind Clicker. Her reaction to

Miranda was much more satisfying.

'Ooooh!' she squeaked, clapping her hand over her mouth, and then, realising there was a camera pointing at her, vainly trying to smooth her hair down. She had taken the braids out long ago.

'Ah, here's someone who recognises me,' said a relieved Miranda, discreetly hustling Clicker out of the way so that she could talk to Gemma.

'I believe you're here to start work on the youth club, is that right?'

'Yes,' said Gemma, looking straight at the camera with a fixed smile which was clearly supposed to display her shiny white teeth to their best advantage. 'That's the idea.'

'Well, I'm here to tell you you're in for a bit of a surprise,' said Miranda. 'Go in and have a look.'

Gemma's film star smile turned to an expression of mystification but obediently she walked over to the front door. It was draped with a bit of old sheeting.

'Move the sheet,' said Miranda.

Gemma did as she was told. 'Oh look, someone's painted the door! What a fantastic colour! That'll save us a bit of work.'

'Go on, go inside,' ordered Miranda.

Gemma turned the handle and went in. Clicker was standing to one side watching.

There was silence for a few seconds, then the most bloodcurdling scream came from the inner recesses of the club. Gemma raced back out of the building shouting at the top of her voice.

'They've done it! It's all been done! Come and look, everyone! Come and see! It's so lovely!' She paused for breath in front of the smugly smiling Miranda. 'I just can't *believe* it.'

'How thick were you?' snorted Sophie from the sofa. 'Surely it was obvious as soon as you saw Miranda Jukes there what she'd been up to.'

'No one guessed,' said Ben, 'it wasn't till you all went in that you realised. Look, they're showing inside now.'

The scene had moved on to the inside of the club. It was indeed quite stunning. The colour scheme had been kept the same but the makeover team had added all sorts of extra little touches which Ben and his helpers hadn't thought of. The computers had been reinstalled, but instead of standing on rather cheap tables they were now slotted into purpose built shelving with spaces for all the paraphernalia that went with them. The serving area had been redesigned, all the plastic bottles had been discarded and soft drinks were now in dispensers with pull handles. Music was playing in the background and climbing plants entwined with discreet light bulbs to festoon the ceiling over the bar. The whole effect was exciting and exotic.

'Quite nice, eh?' said Miranda waving her hand round the room. 'But there's one part we haven't seen yet, a bit which wasn't done by the *Street* team but which was done by a local lad. Let's take a minute to talk to him and find out what it's all about.'

She took a couple of steps backwards holding her hand out and Lee came into view wearing a ragged Eminem T-shirt, frowning with embarrassment and doing his best to look nonchalant.

'This is Lee. He's an artist, aren't you, Lee?'

Lee grunted.

'Lee has created a most unique piece of art, which we're about to see. Can you tell us something about it?'

Lee's face filled the whole screen. He appeared to be tongue-tied.

'What have you actually drawn here?' prompted Miranda patiently. She was obviously used to this sort of thing.

'It's people, innit?' said Lee. 'Like, people who live in

the town and come here. To the club, like.'

'Fascinating,' said Miranda. 'And what gave you the idea?'

'It wasn't me,' said Lee, 'it was him, Jamie, the bloke who died. He'd already done it all in photographs but it all went in the fire, like. So they asked me to paint it instead.'

'What a great idea!' gushed Miranda. 'So, let's have a look.'

The camera panned in on the white wall where Jamie's photos had hung.

Except that the wall was no longer white, it was every colour under the sun, covered with a huge mural depicting the park over the road. The park was full of people involved in different activities, some of them looking straight out from the wall, others in profile and one or two from behind. Every single person there was recognisable as having something to do with the club, many of them were involved in the activities in which Jamie had originally photographed them. Noah was running, Gemma was sprawled on the grass with a magazine, Laura was sitting beside her making a daisy chain and Clicker could be seen from behind on a bench tapping on a laptop. It wasn't exactly a cartoon, nor was it a truly representational painting, yet somehow it seemed to combine qualities of both.

'Sen-sational,' said Miranda, standing back for a better view. 'And the young man Jamie you mentioned, the lad who died. Is he represented here?'

'Yeah,' said Lee jerking a thumb at the side of the picture. 'He's there.'

Jamie had been painted at the bottom right hand corner, taking pictures of the whole scene on his camera. Lee had done him in silhouette, all black paint, so that he seemed to stand out in 3D outside the scene. Although his back was to the room the spiky hair was unmistakably Jamie's and there was no way anyone could doubt it was him.

'And you never knew this boy?' asked Miranda.

'Nah,' said Lee, 'did it from pictures. I had seen him around, though.'

'Remarkable,' breathed Miranda. 'And how would you describe your style? Would you say it was a kind of post-modern art-deco?'

Lee stared at her.

She changed tack. 'The medium is so unusual. Have you done much work on walls before?'

'Oh yeah,' said Lee, 'I do a lot of walls, me.'

'And will you be a regular member of the club?' asked Miranda. 'Are you planning to go on coming here?'

'Dunno,' he said. 'Maybe. They're a bit religious.'

'Well,' said Miranda turning away from him and back to the camera. 'There you have it. Some very happy youngsters. Let's hope there'll be no more catastrophes here and that they'll get years of use from the club. And now back to the studio to hear about next week's programme...'

The Bevans' lounge was filled with a burst of spontaneous applause and a game-show chant of 'Go Miranda, go Miranda.'

'Tea, I think,' said Clare, getting to her feet and stretching.

'I'll help you,' said Clive and the two of them went out to the kitchen leaving the youth group to an excited discussion about the programme: who had thought what and who had looked the most surprised, and whether or not Lee was about to become the latest cult figure on television.

'The police caught up with Max and Dennis, you know,' Noah told Clicker in a quiet moment. 'Apparently someone grassed on them when they were trying to dump some stolen goods in Lancashire.'

'No way. Will they be able to pin the fire on them?'

'Should think it's very likely. Although Lee and friends may have to give evidence and they may be too scared to do that.'

'But it was them who raised the alarm. Perhaps they're planning to change their ways.'

'Yeah. And perhaps pigs will fly.'

People were beginning to leave. Laura wandered into the kitchen to find her parents sitting at the table looking at an old photo album.

'Look at this one, Laura,' said Clare, pointing to a picture of her and Jamie playing in the paddling pool as toddlers. 'You were both so sweet.'

Laura looked over her shoulder. She remembered that afternoon, Jamie had kept splashing her until in the end she had cried and had had to be rescued. Probably Clare had forgotten about all that.

But she hadn't. 'He wasn't very nice to you that day, was he?' she said.

'No. But I suppose I was a terrible wimp.' She looked at the photo for another moment and then said, 'Mum, could Gemma stay the night?'

'Yes, of course. Do you want her in your room?'

'I suppose so. Although it's a dreadful squash in there since I got my new desk.'

'Why don't you both sleep in Jamie's room?' asked Clive. 'You could pull your mattress in there and Gemma could have the bed.'

'Oh, no, I couldn't do that,' protested Laura, shocked at the suggestion.

'Why not? It's over three months since he died. We can't turn his room into a museum and never use it again.'

'No, I know, but I'd feel all funny…'

'I'm not suggesting you move in for good. Just for a

night.' She glanced at him and realised with surprise that he was pleading with her. 'Go on, Laura, it would help us too.'

'We–ell. Perhaps. If Gemma doesn't mind.' She still looked dubious.

'Just try it. You can always move back to your room if you really feel too strange.'

Laura and Gemma sat in their night-clothes at opposite ends of Jamie's bed and sipped Laura's latest milkshake concoction through straws. Gemma had asked Laura's mum if she might have one of Jamie's old T-shirts and she was wearing it now; it nearly came down to her knees. It was extra large and had his swimming team logo across the front.

The milkshake was made from all sorts of interesting ingredients including strawberry cordial and pineapple chunks.

'Wicked,' said Gemma after the first slurp. 'You should patent these.'

'Mmm,' agreed Laura. They sat in companionable silence.

'It feels really weird, being here in Jamie's room,' said Gemma, looking at her surroundings. 'There's still lots of his stuff in here. It's kind of spooky. Not in a ghostly kind of way,' she said hurriedly, seeing Laura's face, 'I meant spooky in the feeling that he's not really gone. Do you feel that?'

'Not as much as I used to,' said Laura, remembering the first few days when she'd kept expecting him to walk through the door. That happened a lot less often now.

But something different was on her mind at the moment. 'Gem, can I tell you something I've never told anyone else?'

'Sure. Spit it out.'

'Well, it's just that – I don't quite know how to say this – but sometimes I think – sometimes I think Mum and Dad wished it was me that had died and not Jamie.'

She'd said it. Even as she spoke she thought how petty and whingey the words sounded.

'Course you do,' said Gemma calmly. 'Bound to.'

'What do you mean?' asked Laura, amazed.

'It's not a new feeling, believe me. I've been there, done that and got the T-shirt. I know for a fact that Steve loves Jodie more than me, and you can't blame him when you think that she's his real daughter and I'm not. And occasionally, just occasionally, I think Mum feels the same way. I mean Jodie's so cute and Mum loves Steve. Whereas my dad treated her really badly, and I guess sometimes she looks at me and thinks of him.'

Laura struggled to get her head round what Gemma was saying. 'So how on earth do you cope with it?'

'I don't always. Sometimes it really gets to me. But I decided ages ago that if I let it take over I would end up so bitter and twisted no one would ever want to speak to me again. The thing is, it's probably mostly in my head and isn't true at all. It's just that you can't be sure. Parents aren't perfect. Why don't you talk to the school counsellor sometime?'

As a matter of fact Mrs Green had suggested this to Laura only last week, but Laura had stalled, not sure that she wanted to talk about her innermost feelings to a stranger.

But talking to Gemma was OK. 'Are you saying I should just live with thinking that they loved Jamie best?'

'No, course I'm not saying that. I'm just saying don't let it take over your whole life when it's very unlikely to be true. You know, Laura, you may not realise it, but it's obvious to any outsider that without you your mum and dad would find it far harder to handle Jamie's death. They really need you. And not just 'cause you're the one that's left but 'cause you have this kind of laid-backness that's special to you. You give them something no one else could.'

Laura thought about this. Then she said, 'You're not really the airhead you'd like us all to believe, are you?'

'Indeed I am,' replied Gemma in insulted tones.

'You know that stuff Simon said about knowing God's love through our friends?'

'Yes. I remember.'

'Well, you're it,' said Laura.

They finished their drinks and climbed under their duvets, Gemma in Jamie's bed and Laura on the mattress on the floor.

'We haven't cleaned our teeth,' said Gemma drowsily.

'Who cares?' said Laura. She suddenly felt very irresponsible. 'He is still there, you know, Gem. God I mean. I thought he didn't exist any more, but I know he is still there. I can't prove it, but I can just kind of feel it.'

'Mmmm,' said Gemma.

'Gem?'

'What now?'

'Did you mean what you said at the service? About fancying Jamie and everything?'

'Mmmm,' said Gemma again, adding in distant tones, 'now would I lie about something like that? In front of all those people? I don't think so.'

'You're weird,' said Laura, but Gemma was snoring.

She lay awake a little longer, thinking about Jamie and the club and everything that had happened over the last few months. She knew there was still a very long way to go before life would seem anywhere near normal, in fact nothing would ever be quite the same again. She knew that she herself had changed a lot and that the way she was with her mum and dad had changed too. She was an only child now. That meant all her parents' expectations would be concentrated on her, quite a scary thought.

But there were things to look forward to as well.

She wondered if Lee would start coming to the Halfway House. He'd be bound to drag Vinny and Robbie along with him, and perhaps others of his friends as well. What a challenge *that* would be.

Laura slept.